CW01084955

The Key

Sarah Sheridan

BLOODHOUND
— BOOKS —

First published in 2023 by Bloodhound Books.

www.bloodhoundbooks.com

Print ISBN: 978-1-5040-8629-5

For Diane,
Here's to many more cocktail evenings

Chapter One

I only went to Godwyne Castle to write a book. I had no way of knowing – as I parked my car on the expansive gravel drive – that my mere presence at the Trengrouse family seat would set off such a series of murderous events. And to think, the whole project had started off so promisingly...

I peered along the dimly lit corridor. I was pretty sure I was in the right place. I'd followed the instructions of Godwyne Castle's manager, Mr Derek Brentwood, to the best of my abilities, weaving my way through the labyrinth of rooms and passages until I was somewhere on the second floor of the east wing of the vast, run-down building.

'You'll find the Upper Library behind the last door at the end of the Green Corridor, Miss Haythorpe,' Mr Brentwood had said in his dry tones.

Walking along, I passed rows of closed doors on either side. There was a cold, dusty feel to this part of the building, and I had the sense that it had been barely used for centuries. I reached the very last door and the sign on its front indicated that I'd found what I was looking for. I placed my hand on the doorknob and turned it; expectant and excited. This room was going to become my second home for the foreseeable future. I was desperately hoping that it would hold all the material that I needed for the research for my next book.

As a writer of non-fiction books I loved it when my creations did well; adored it when they rose up the Amazon rankings shortly after publication, and most of all relished browsing reviews from readers who'd really enjoyed what I'd written. But this time I had an even more pressing desire for this next work to do well. My ten-year-old niece, Gabrielle, had been born with cystic fibrosis and had recently become very ill. My sister Penny knew that Gabby's best chance for treatment lay in America, where a new triple combination therapy for the mutation that her daughter had was being trialled. I'd spent most of my last advance on rent for my house – before Gabby became so poorly – and had just enough left to survive on for the foreseeable future. Penny was a single mother who worked part time as a teaching assistant, there was no way she could afford the cost of such a trip. But I would never be able to forget the desperation in her voice as she told me about the treatment that Gabby so badly needed, but that she had no way to pay for.

'I just don't know what to do, Grace,' she kept saying through sobs. 'What will happen to Gabby if I can't get her over there?'

Both our parents had – sadly – passed away years before from different types of cancer, and although Penny would never ask me directly, I knew that I was her best bet for funding Gabby's treatment. The only way I could really help Penny and Gabby was to write such a stunning book about early twentieth century aristocracy – with the Trengrouse family from Godwyne Castle in the wilds of southernmost Cornwall as my case studies – that I could secure a big enough advance to help fund Gabby's treatment.

At my career stage this was not an impossible plan. For the last ten years, since the age of twenty-six, I'd been immersed in writing about various historical subjects, managing to garner a rather wonderful group of readers who were loyal to my books. Over the last four years each new release had sold especially well, in part thanks to my wonderful journalist friend – Kim Ulrich – writing glowing articles about them. I had to admit though, that being a writer was a tenuous way to live, as I'd feel flush when the advances and royalties came in, and rather poor and struggling when they'd run out. But that was all part of my job, and it was one that I absolutely loved to do – I wouldn't have it any other way. Although all the hours I spent bent over my laptop did have an impact on my love life – or lack of it. I hadn't had a relationship since Stuart moved out eighteen months ago – citing the fact that I put my writing before him (probably true). But that was okay, I needed to get this project finished before I worried about dating again.

And my wonderful agent, Daiyu Zhang, knew about my family situation – I'd blurted it all out to her one day after breaking down crying during a meeting in her office – and had promised to find a great publisher and advance for the new title.

'Leave it with me,' Daiyu had said, handing me a box of tissues. 'I'll get the best deal I can for you.'

So now all I had to do was to write the manuscript, and make sure it was of the highest possible quality...

Entering the library, I took in the endless rows of books, the neatly stacked boxes of files, an old-looking cabinet that was crammed with ancient pots and broken ceramic things, and the amount of dust that covered everything. The files would hold the documents that I was interested in; the family archives, papers, letters, and everything else that would help me to bring the Trengrouse family's history to life for my readers. And of course, I was hoping to find some information out about the tantalizing Trengrouse family secret that I'd read about on the web... the myth of their buried treasure. Now that would be a *great* hook for readers...

Oh my goodness, I thought, overwhelmed for a second or two. *This is going to be a big job. There's so much to go through.* Granted, research was my thing, but this collection – on first inspection – seemed even more enormous than usual.

But as I wandered closer to the first row of shelves, I realised that my job had been made slightly easier by whoever the kind person was that had already catalogued all the documents. Each box was labelled in swirly, copperplate writing, displaying the dates of the papers kept inside. By the yellowing of the labels this was a job that had obviously been done years ago.

Wondering if this cataloguing extended up to the modern day, I walked round to the last row of shelves at the back of the room. But here I found the files and papers had just been stacked higgledy-piggledy along the wooden shelves; no order or labels to be seen. Goodness knows how anyone would find anything they needed among that mess. Luckily, they were the wrong century for me – my interest lay firmly in the nineteen hundreds. Retracing my steps, I studied the intervening shelves until I found what I was looking for. The last neatly recorded label by whomever the person was who'd shown such an interest in ordering the family documents, read: *Trengrouse Family 1955 – 1959*. Presumably this abrupt end to the organising would give a clue as to who had been behind it. Perhaps they'd done it up until they became too ill to hold a pen? Who knows? But that was just my inquisitive mind talking. Finding out who'd labelled the archives wasn't a pressing necessity, it could wait for another day. Whereas starting the book was...

I circled the old desks that had been placed in the centre of the library, choosing my pew for the next few weeks. As I did so, I contemplated the fact that what made this job even more interesting and compelling was that I was somehow very distantly related to the Trengrouse family; a detail that had been behind my choice to use them as case studies for the book. My parents had brought us up with this knowledge, told to us in a light-hearted and fun kind of way.

'Just think,' Mum would laugh, 'if our ancestors had made different choices, we'd be living in a castle today, girls.'

And then Penny and I would giggle, and dress up in princess outfits and imagine what life would have been like if that had been the case. It had never been a big deal as I'd grown up, more of an interesting anecdote to tell friends. And we'd had a wonderful childhood in our three-bed semi in Chislehurst, Kent.

'Ooh, guess what? I'm related to an old aristocratic family.'

'Why aren't you loaded then?'

'Not sure. Someone somewhere probably got disinherited...'

I wasn't even clear about how exactly we were linked to the Trengrouses, it seemed to be a convoluted story of many cousins five times removed, or something equally obscure. I just liked having the connection, especially now as I was about to begin the book. It made me feel more invested in the project, and I fancied that perhaps an old, long-dead ancestor was looking out for me in the castle, and would point me in the direction of the best documents, for Gabby's sake.

Right Grace, I told myself, placing my laptop bag on my chosen desk. *Enough of the musing. It's time to get started...*

Chapter Two

I was immersed in a diary from the first file I'd chosen to take off the front row of shelves, labelled *Trengrouse Family 1900 – 1902*, when the library door suddenly swung wide open.

'What are you doing in here?' a woman's voice, full of affront, said.

'Er...' I turned, trying to quickly get my head back into the right century. The corridor had seemed so quiet, I hadn't been expecting any kind of company. Meeting the gaze of the interloper – as I thought of her – into my space, I took in her appearance. Shortish, over sixty, lined face, not smiling. Grey hair pulled back tightly. 'I'm Grace Haythorpe. I've been given permission by Mr Brentwood to research in here. I'm writing a book about the Trengrouse family's history.' I tucked a strand of my long brown hair behind my ear.

'Are you indeed?' the woman said. 'No one's allowed into this part of the castle, usually. And I should know, I've worked here for over forty years.'

'Ah,' I said, understanding. I'd done a fair bit of reading

around Godwyne Castle before my arrival and knew that during the summer months bits of it were open to the public on certain days of the week. It was partly how they funded the upkeep of the old pile. Maybe this lady thought I was an errant sightseer who'd just randomly wandered into an off-limits area on a day when the castle was closed. 'No it's all right, I'm a writer. I'm going to be working here for at least a month, maybe more.'

'I see,' the woman said. 'I'm surprised the family gave you permission to come into this library. Mr Brentwood would have had to ask them. I haven't seen a Trengrouse in here for decades. I, of course, walk around the castle every day, to make sure that everything is in order. I'm Margaret Taylor, the housekeeper. You can call me Mrs Taylor. Lunch is at 1pm sharp. If you're working here now, I suppose you better join us.'

'Do you eat with the Trengrouses?' I said.

'No, Miss Haythorpe.' The woman looked disapproving. 'That would never happen; just imagine us eating with a lord and lady. Lunch at 1pm is for the staff. The Trengrouse family – or those that are around – eat at 12.15.'

'Oh of course,' I said, feeling silly, a warm blush spreading over my cheeks. 'Thank you, I'd love to come and dine with you.' I'd just brought a couple of sandwiches with me; the thought that I'd actually be invited for lunch by the staff had never crossed my mind.

Mrs Taylor nodded, and left the library, without a hint of a smile on her face.

Interesting, I thought, turning back to the old papers in front of me. *The atmosphere in this place is definitely not warm, and neither – it seems – are the people who work here*. I'd spent time researching in many manor houses and grand stately homes across Britain, as I compiled information for each book. And over the years I'd begun to see how the feeling in a house, and the attitudes of the staff there, often reflected the temperaments of the family who owned the place. For example, everything about Chatslane in Surrey exuded warmth, and when I'd met the living relatives of the Burnett family who lived in a small section of the place, I'd understood why. They'd been so hospitable and kind, and had taken a genuine interest in my work. And their staff had made me feel very welcome, constantly bringing me tea and coffee, and had only had good things to say about their employers. The sunny, gorgeously decorated rooms in Chatslane had furthered this notion of cordiality.

What then, did the cold, dark corridors of Godwyne Castle and the standoffish nature of Mrs Taylor herald about the Trengrouse family? In photos the building looked like a magnificent pile, but when I saw it in real life for the first time that morning a shiver had gone down my spine. The Gothic spires looked impressive in sunlight, but what atmosphere would the building give off when the weather was rainy or misty? Time would tell, but I had a feeling that I'd get more of an insight into how things were run at Godwyne during lunch. Talking to the people who worked at my place of interest was always invaluable; one way or other these conversations always seemed to further my subject knowledge. Although if Mrs Taylor's attitude towards me was anything to go by, lunch might very well be a rather frosty affair. Oh well, at least I was warned now...

Bending down over the diary in front of me, I found the point that I'd been up to. It had been written by one of my long-lost ancestors in September 1900, his name inscribed on the inside of the cover: Archie Trengrouse.

Brought up the subject of repairs with Cordelia again, I read. *No luck. She seems determined to refurbish the London house.*

Told her that this was rot, that Godwyne needs fixing more urgently than the London place needs new drapes. Damp is spreading throughout, and many of the windows need fixing. Certain rooms are altogether in a state of disrepair, and two of the stables need looking at. But she's not interested in this castle at all. Never has been, can't understand my digs either. Doesn't understand what I see of interest in the old monastery ruins, or in any other part of the grounds. No sense of the history of the place. Well, the conversation went the usual way and ended with her tears. Damn family, they're all the same.

Wow, I thought, leaning back in my chair. *If this page is anything to go by, it seems that I'm going to get a very good insight into the problems of the family, as well as into their social scene.* Archie's wife Cordelia Trengrouse's legendary socialising was really what I was looking for; she'd often made headlines due to the extravagant parties that she threw at the Trengrouses' London residence, as well as for her connections to all the important society figures of the day. I planned to look for her own journals, but being of a curious nature I was finding Archie's words compelling. And it was so thrilling to have my own – very distant – ancestors coming to life like this; however removed they actually were from me. I knew – from the research that I'd done before arriving at Godwyne – that Archibald Trengrouse was the great, great grandfather of the current heir to the castle – Edward – who lived somewhere in the sprawling building with his wife Susannah. I knew that Edward and Susannah had two sons, who were now in their twenties, although I didn't know whether the boys still lived at Godwyne too. Archie had had one sister and one brother, and I was pretty sure that my own bloodline stemmed in some way from a much more distant ancestor. My own common relative with the current Trengrouses would be found in the dim and distant past, I was sure of it; a common great grandmother or something from hundreds of years ago. If, in fact, the tale turned out to be true. It would be exciting if my research eventually uncovered a bit about my own family line, and I was secretly hoping that it would, just so I could tell Penny.

Charles FitzConnor says that profits from his mine are up again, for the fifth year in a row. How perfectly wonderful for him...

Ah yes, I thought. 1900 was still the golden age for aristocracy who were lucky enough to have profitable coal mines on their land. Although – as I knew from previous research – the first miners' strike in 1912 heralded what would become the beginning of the end for private landowners, as after a long and convoluted battle between the government, coal owners and miners that ran for decades, the collieries were nationalised in 1947, bringing an end to the fat royalties that landowners had creamed off the coal business for years. I knew that the Godwyne estate had never been mined for coal, however I made a note of Charles FitzConnor's name in case it proved relevant in the future.

I turned the page and a photo fell out. I knew at once that it was Archie, and turning it over confirmed this fact; his name was written on the back. A young, handsome, smiling face beamed out at me. Strong chin, an aristocratic nose and laughter lines around the eyes. He was wearing smart clothes, and the hat on his head finished off the look. He looked so carefree, so wonderfully at ease with the world. He must have been one hell of a catch back then.

I carried on reading. *Cordy says that the Carmichaels are coming to stay again on Saturday, and that I'm to take them out hunting. Good Lord, what on earth am I going to find to talk about this time? Personally I'd rather stay inside and talk to Beatrice...* I stopped again. I knew – from my previous research about the family – that Beatrice was Archie's firstborn of four, a daughter who'd arrived in the world in 1899, when Archie was just twenty-one. I was finding this insight into Archie's personality fascinating, not least because it conflicted so much with his public image. I'd already read, before arriving, that early twentieth century society papers had been full of the glamorous Cordelia Trengrouse, who often had her husband Archie by her side. Lots of these papers were now readily accessible online, and before arriving at Godwyne Castle I'd pored over the black and white photos of the two of them, admiring Cordelia's beauty and Archie's self-assured smile. They'd been among the most popular and influential figures in Britain at the time, always attending the right parties in the most fashionable outfits. And the Carmichaels – who Archie was referring to in his diary, Vita and Edgar – had been part of the same glittering set. I'd come across them many times before, when writing other non-fiction books.

Perhaps naively, I'd presumed that Archie was as enthusiastic about socialising as his wife was. That they made the perfect socialite couple. So why, then, was Archie writing in his private journal that he'd rather play with his one-year-old daughter than spend time entertaining his friends the Carmichaels? Did this outwardly social man have an introvert side? It wouldn't be the first time that someone kept up appearances for the sake of class and reputation. Some of the party set of those days seemed to relish their lifestyle, whereas a few seemed to find it an empty and vacuous way of living. Perhaps Archie privately adhered to the second of these two sets, while outwardly keeping up appearances for the sake of the family?

I became lost in Archie's diary again, to the point where I

lost track of time. When I did eventually check my phone, I saw that it was 1.05pm.

Oh shit, I thought, hastily closing the journal and standing up. *I'm already late for lunch, and on my first day here. What the hell is Mrs Taylor going to have to say about that?*

Chapter Three

It occurred to me, as I retraced my steps back through the passages to the main marble staircase, that I'd been so startled by Mrs Taylor's arrival in the library that I'd forgotten to ask her exactly where the staff lunch took place. I had no idea where I was supposed to now go. The castle was like an indoor maze, a vast concoction of interconnecting rooms and corridors with countless outbuildings, and I doubted that I'd ever learn my way around.

Walking out through the main front door – taking in the sight of the beautifully kept, expansive grounds – then trotting down the stone steps, I caught sight of a man on a ride-on mower.

'Hi,' I called. 'Excuse me?'

He turned, and slowly drove the machine towards me.

'You couldn't direct me to the staff lunch room, could you?' I said, walking closer. 'I'm already late and I have no idea where I'm going. It's my first day working here.'

'You must be that writer, Grace Haythorpe,' he said, the edges of his blue eyes crinkling. He flipped a mop of golden hair out of his eyes.

'Er, yes,' I said, feeling somewhat taken aback. 'How did you know?'

'There's not many secrets at Godwyne,' he said with a grin. 'Not among the staff anyway. We all rub along together quite nicely – usually. The family, however, is a different matter altogether. I'm Jesse Benson, I'm the groundsman here. Nice to meet you, Grace.'

I nodded, taking in my new acquaintance. *Thirties,* I decided. *Kind manner, rather attractive, and from the look of the grounds, good at his job. Thank God someone here seems friendly...*

'And yes, you are late for lunch,' Jesse said with a smile. 'Our Mrs Taylor – Margaret – will no doubt have some serious words to say to you about that. But don't mind her too much, her bark is much worse than her bite.'

I nodded again.

'Mrs Taylor and I have already met,' I said. 'Up in the library on the second floor. I don't think she was too impressed to find me in there actually.'

'Old Margaret is the longest serving one of us here,' Jesse said, turning the engine off. 'Runs the place, and thinks she owns it half the time. But she's good at what she does, and the family wouldn't be able to cope without her, I reckon. Now, let's get you to lunch; if you walk fast you might just get there in time for pudding...'

Jesse climbed off the mower and ushered me round to the left of the bleak, grey castle. I took the chance to have another look at the rolling grounds that spread away from the castle, the undulating lines of the fields and meadows, the copses, woods, lakes, small valleys and hills. It really was a sensational setting, and one that was as beautiful as the castle was stark.

Then I caught sight of a small, brownish-grey cat walking slowly towards us over the grass.

'Ah, here comes Hobnob,' Jesse said with a grin. 'Belongs to Mary, our resident cook. Named after her favourite biscuits, apparently.'

Hobnob arrived at my feet and began rubbing herself against my ankles. I bent down to stroke her, and noticed that she had the most enormous eyes I'd ever seen on a cat. They were peering up at me, the size of saucers.

'She's lovely,' I said, standing up again.

Jesse pointed to a door at the end of the grey stone wall.

'Old servants' entrance,' he said with a grin. 'And still used by the likes of us today. I've already had my food, I eat it quick as there's always so much work to do here. I've got to get on now, someone's been digging holes in the grounds again – damn nuisance. Must be an outsider as the family always tells me what they're up to. I hope the lot of them have left enough food for you. And remember what I said, don't take too much notice of Margaret Taylor. She's like one of the paintings in the castle; invaluable but old and very stark.'

I snorted, thanked him for his help, took a deep breath and set off towards the door.

'How nice of you to join us, Miss Haythorpe.' Mrs Taylor's words reached me even before I saw her. I couldn't help wondering if she'd been slightly looking forward to me arriving so that she could say that very phrase. Gazing around the dark stone room, my eyes adjusting to the dim light, I spotted her sitting at the head of a wooden trestle table that ran down the centre. Three other people were there too. 'There's not much food left, but that's what happens when you're late. What's left is on the sideboard over there. The plates and cutlery are on the shelf above. Go and help yourself and then come and sit down with the rest of us.'

I obediently did what she said, flashbacks of being told off by an old headmistress coming to mind, and found that there was in fact ample food left for a good lunch. I levered a slice of cold meat pie on my plate, added some salad, and then made my way to an empty chair at the other end of the table to where Mrs Taylor sat.

'Water jug and glasses are over there,' she said, pointing. 'Go and get yourself a drink. There are no airs and graces down here, we all muck in and look after ourselves at mealtimes.'

'Thank you, Mrs Taylor,' I said. 'I'll get one in a minute.'

Faces were turning towards me. A young, pretty lady, an older woman, and the manager of the castle who'd met me when I'd arrived, Derek Brentwood.

'Hi,' I said, cutting up the pie. 'I'm Grace Haythorpe, I'll be working at the castle over the next few weeks. I'm writing a book about the Trengrouse family.'

'Derek's just told us,' the older woman said. She gave me a smile. 'Margaret said you gave her a right fright when she saw you in the upper library earlier. I'm Mary, I'm the cook here. It's nice to meet you, Grace.'

I smiled back at her.

'Well, I had no idea that Miss Haythorpe was going to be there, did I?' Mrs Taylor sniffed. 'Mr Brentwood has only just told us why she's here. I could have done with that particular bit of knowledge yesterday.' She glared at Mr Brentwood.

'You weren't in yesterday, Margaret,' Mr Brentwood said with a sigh. 'Sunday is always your day off. I told you as soon as I saw you this morning.'

'Yes, well that was twenty minutes too late,' Mrs Taylor said.

'Anyway,' Mary said, rolling her eyes at me in mock frustration. 'This is Zara, she does the accounts.'

The young woman gave me a grin and waved her hand. She was pretty, I noticed, in a delicate kind of way. Probably about my age, maybe a year or two older.

'And then there's Jesse, who's the gardener. That's the lot of us that are left here now. What with all the cutbacks the Trengrouses had to make last year...'

'Yes, well I don't think we need to go into those now, do we, Mary?' Mrs Taylor's gaze was sharp. 'I mean, family business is just that. It's...'

The door banged open and a man's voice shouted:

'Granny? Granny? Where the fuck are you?'

'Oh God,' Zara muttered. 'It's Will.'

A tanned, muscly, twenty-something man strode into the dining room.

'Hey, you lot,' he said in cut-glass tones. 'Have you seen my grandmother anywhere?'

His gaze came to rest on me.

'I know who you are,' he said, his voice getting louder. 'You're that bloody writer. You've got a damn cheek coming here, if you ask me. Just don't expect any help from me or my family with your silly little scribblings. And if you want my advice, you should leave the estate now, before you get properly started. And burn any notes you've already made.'

He turned and exited the room, slamming the door shut behind him.

Chapter Four

As I laid down my knife and fork, I noticed that my hands were shaking.

'Don't take any notice of Will,' Zara said in a low voice, leaning towards me. 'He's nothing but a brutish bully. I try and stay away from him as much as possible. His brother, Howard, is much nicer to deal with, as you'll find out.'

'Now, now, Zara, let's not have any talk against the family,' Mrs Taylor said. But when I looked at her, I saw a look of worry in her eyes.

'Are you okay, dear?' Mary said, turning towards me. 'Young Will always talks to us lowly members of staff like that. I reckon he was born with a silver spoon shoved so far down his throat it got stuck, which explains why he's been in a bad mood ever since...'

'Mary.' Mrs Taylor spat out the word. 'That is *enough*.'

'I must go now.' Mr Brentwood stood up and took his plate over to a sink in the corner, as though nothing had happened. He must be used to all this banter and quarrelling, I thought, watching him turn towards the table again. 'Goodbye, all,' he said, and left the room.

I managed to give Mary and Zara small smiles. I was feeling very grateful for their kind words. Will's outburst had shocked me. I mean, I'd encountered rude rich people before when I'd researched other books; disgruntled members of families who weren't particularly nice to anyone. But Will's attack had felt rather direct, as though he actually had something against me personally. But how could that be? I was surprised he even knew who I was, and that I wrote books for a living. In the past, I'd often spent weeks reading through old family documents without actually meeting one of the family members once. It was easier like that. Will's vitriol had really thrown me. I was no longer hungry, I realised.

'I must go off and check the entrance hall,' Mrs Taylor said, glancing at the clock on the wall. She stood up. 'The family has visitors arriving at half past two. If Jesse hasn't put fresh flowers in the vases yet, he's going to have some explaining to do.'

She left the dining room.

'God, is it nearly two o'clock already?' Zara said, getting to her feet. 'I've got to get the books ready for their meeting.'

She hurried off.

So then, it was just me and Mary the cook sitting opposite each other at the table.

'The Trengrouses are a funny lot,' Mary said. 'And the staff aren't much better.' She winked at me. I grinned back. I was starting to feel normal again; the sting of Will's words losing their potency. I picked up my fork.

'So do Will and Howard live here at the castle then?' I said, skewering a piece of pie.

'Yes, the whole family is still here,' Mary said. She shook her head. 'They're a rum lot. Will's the worst, arrogant prat. Can't seem to keep his mouth shut. Howard's okay – always friendly and polite to everyone, and his wife Mimi seems to be a good sort. Don't know her very well. Edward and Sukie – the boys' parents – stay out of the way most of the time. I think they're as sick of Will as the rest of us are. Although Sukie can be... well, you'll find out for yourself soon enough I suppose. And you'll see the grandmother, Alexandra – Edward's mum – wandering about from time to time. Losing her marbles now, poor dear. Oh,' her nose wrinkled. 'I almost forgot. There's Helena, the boys' cousin, too. She came to stay for a few months last year and never left. Silly airhead if you ask me, always wants Uncle Edward to hand out an endless stream of money to her. Just has to bat her eyelids at him and he gives her whatever she wants.'

I nodded, chewing.

'So there's seven Trengrouses still living here,' I said through my food. 'More than I thought.'

'Yep, and that's seven too many if you ask me,' Mary said with a chuckle. 'Only joking, like I said – some of them aren't too bad. It's that Will you need to stay away from; nothing but bad news, that boy. Now, I must get on. Got to get all these plates washed up one way or another. Take your time though, dear, no rush. You just finish what's on your plate, and I'll come back for it in a bit.'

She pottered off through a door at the back of the room that I hadn't spotted before. Hobnob arrived through an open window, jumped down, and started cleaning herself, one leg stuck high above her head.

I worked my way through the rest of the slice of pie, which turned out to be absolutely delicious. A wood panel above was decorated with what looked like a map of the castle grounds. 'Old Stables', 'Icehouse' and 'Monastery Ruins' were just some of the tantalising labels adorning it. The way the map was laid out made the estate look like a place from medieval times; it was intriguing, and made me want to walk around the grounds and explore them myself. Discover all the different features – old and new – that were scattered about.

'There you are,' a thin voice said. The pronunciation smacked of old aristocracy.

I turned.

An old woman with long, wispy white hair down to her waist, was standing at the door. Her face, now ancient, still held memories of beauty. She was as thin as a stick, and was wearing only a long nightdress. I knew at once – from the numerous photos I'd browsed through on the internet before arriving – who she was. Lady Alexandra Trengrouse, mother to the heir, Edward.

'I know who you are,' Alexandra said to me, stepping forward. 'You're the writer girl. I need to speak to you.'

'Lady Trengrouse?' I said.

'Call me Alexandra, Grace,' she said. 'Listen...'

'Granny?' a man's voice called. It didn't have the anger of Will's tone. So it must be Howard's?

'Come to see me tonight.' Alexandra leant forwards, her eyes now wide. 'They'll try and stop me talking to you. But you must know. It's for your own safety. Don't forget what I said. Come and find me. Follow the white roses and you'll know where to go...'

Chapter Five

'Found you, Granny,' the man's voice said.

He soon came into view, putting his arm round Alexandra's tiny waist.

'Hello there,' he said to me with a smile. 'I'm Howard, the nicer son. Apologies in advance if you've already met Will. You must be Grace Haythorpe. Wonderful to meet you. Welcome to Godwyne. Now,' he said, looking at his grandmother. 'Let's get you back to your room, shall we, Granny? You'll catch your death if you keep insisting on adventuring around in your nightdress.'

As he led her away, Alexandra turned and stared at me. There was something imploring in her eyes.

Well, I thought, staring after them. *This really is the most extraordinary family that I've ever encountered. And trust me to be distantly related to them; not that any of them will have the faintest clue about that – they must have hundreds of vaguely related cousins littered around the country. So, Alexandra wants me to go to her room later this evening? Mary said she was losing her mind, and judging from the fact she was just wandering around in her nightdress, that might well be the case. Funny though, because when I looked into her eyes I could see a strong sanity in them. But no doubt Mrs Taylor would have me thrown out of Godwyne if she found me anywhere near the family's private quarters. And as for Will, I dread to think what he'd do...*

I placed my knife, fork and plate in the sink as I'd seen the others do, had a quick drink of water, and then made my way back through the castle's maze of corridors and rooms to the Upper Library.

My head was reeling as I sat down. So much had happened since I'd gone down for lunch, and it was all so bewildering. How did I even begin to make sense of it all? Of everything that had been said?

First, there was Will. Why was my presence at Godwyne making him so enraged? What was it he'd said – 'You've got a damn cheek coming here... If you want my advice, you should leave the estate now... And burn any notes you've already made.' What did he mean, I had a cheek coming to the castle? I was just an author, a recorder of history. I wasn't planning on writing about Will – or any of the other living family – at all; all my subjects were long dead. And he didn't want me to even be on the grounds. Wanted me to destroy anything I'd already noticed and recorded. But why? Unless... there were some sort of family secrets that he didn't want exposed. But what kind of family secrets from the past would still be relevant in the present day? The fanciful myth about the buried treasure? Well, that was already a known fact, you could find information about it in old newspapers, if you knew where to look. Or maybe, I thought, it was just part of Will's aggressive personality, to go round talking to strangers like that. That's what everyone else had seemed to think; none of them had been shocked by his outburst. Hadn't Zara said that he was always a bully? Maybe I shouldn't take his words too personally.

And then there was the surprise visit from old Alexandra in

her nightdress. Her mysterious plea for me to come and visit her in her room this evening. I mean, even if I wanted to it would be absolutely inappropriate for me to go sneaking into the family's private quarters like that. It would be totally unprofessional, and if word got out about that it could tarnish my reputation as a writer. No, I couldn't even afford to entertain the idea. And yet, she'd been so insistent. She'd genuinely seemed to want to impart some sort of information to me. 'For my own safety,' she'd said. What on earth could she possibly mean? Perhaps Mary the cook was right, and Alexandra was losing her mind. Maybe I'd just been today's subject, the receiver of her wandering thoughts. But I wasn't entirely convinced she was all that senile; I'd seen an unmistakable intelligence in her eyes...

Howard had seemed nice, much more palatable than his brother. He was stockier and shorter than Will, with a broader forehead, calmer eyes and an air of quiet authority about him. Both of them had a shock of dark red hair. Thank goodness Howard was the elder of the two, the one who'd one day be head of Godwyne Castle. I couldn't help thinking its future would be in much safer hands with him, than with the volatile Will...

But then, I thought, opening Archie's diary again, *perhaps I was reading too much into everything that had gone on. I hadn't had much sleep last night, been too anxious about getting up early and setting off on the long drive down to Cornwall. I'd probably have a different perspective on everything tomorrow.* Thinking of sleep, I'd have to go and find Mrs Taylor soon, and ask her to show me to my room. When I'd applied to the castle for access to the records, I'd been given the option of boarding there for the duration of my research, at a very reasonable fee per week. I'd jumped at the chance; Godwyne was so remote that travelling back and forth from my apartment in Hammersmith, West London, was unthinkable. And I just didn't have the funds to lodge in a nearby hotel or B & B for any extended length of time. When Mr Brentwood had met me at the door that morning, he'd explained that my room was still being cleaned, and would be ready for me later on in the day. But it was only early afternoon, and I still had time to do a lot more work before going to find the housekeeper. So I had to try and push all of today's events out of my mind now, and concentrate hard on the diary in front of me...

Shafts of April sunlight were illuminating the swirly words. I stared down at them, hoping to find a good anecdote about Archie and Cordelia's famous socialising, a story that would really open the book with a bang. Perhaps they had dined with very famous people in their day? Or even better, been associated with some sort of scandal? Or even a hint about the treasure... Anything that whet the readers appetites for more would be just the thing.

3rd October 1900, I read. *Cordy reports trouble with her new maid. She won't take orders from the older staff, apparently. It's the fourth one she's had in the last two years, Lord knows why the servants harbour such petty jealousies towards each other. Took another look at the expenses. Not good. Something must be done about them or Godwyne will fall into trouble. Well, more trouble than we're experiencing already, although the rest of the family seem blind to it.* Hmm, I thought. Another reference to not all being well financially for the Trengrouses during this period; Archie had mentioned something about it in his previous diary entry, hadn't he? Well this was news to me; I hadn't come across any record of this in the research I'd done before coming to Godwyne. Perhaps Archie managed to resolve whatever the problem was, and to keep the matter private? I read on:

Cordy and I are expected at the Dorchester's ball in London tomorrow night. It will be a late affair, no doubt full of the usual twittering women and boring men banging on about their latest assets. When will she have had her fill of this kind of thing? I suppose we must go, however...

A noise made me stop and look up. It was a soft, whirring sound, something you might expect to hear in an office, but incongruent to my dusty old castle surroundings. I looked around, wondering where it was coming from. As I looked above me, I saw that something on the ceiling was glinting in the sunlight. *How strange. What can that possibly be?* I wondered. *A fire alarm, perhaps?* I stood up, and saw that it was a small, box-like contraption that had been securely fixed to a high wooden beam.

I decided to stand on a chair to take a closer look at it. As I did so, the soft whirring happened again, and to my complete surprise I saw a lens retract in the centre of the box. It wasn't a fire alarm, it was a camera. *Had someone been watching me since my arrival at Godwyne?*

Chapter Six

'Ah, Mr Brentwood, there you are,' I said, feeling quite out of breath. It had taken me nearly twenty minutes to find him, there was so much castle to search through. Even with the natural light coming through the windows, it was an imposing place. Not at all cosy or warm. There was something distinctly unfriendly about the lack of any attempt at an inviting ambience. *If it was mine,* I thought, *I'd definitely soften the atmosphere with some lighter furnishings, some attractive carpets and curtains.* But as it was, it seemed cold and somewhat unfriendly and smelt faintly of damp. As though its soul was suffocating; mouldering away. Definitely not a place I'd like to live in long term.

I'd eventually located Mr Brentwood in one of the cellars, where he appeared to be doing an inventory of the hundreds of dusty bottles of wine.

'Miss Haythorpe,' he said, turning towards me. 'How can I be of assistance?'

'Well, I just wanted to check something really,' I said. 'This might sound silly, but I just noticed a camera above me in the

Upper Library, and I had the strangest feeling that someone was watching me through it. Is this normal for Godwyne?'

Mr Brentwood's lips cracked into a thin smile.

'Yes.' He nodded slightly. 'Quite normal and nothing to worry about. The family had a rather high-tech security system installed after the break-in last year. Now each room has its own camera, and there are monitors in the office where we can view what's going on around the castle. I believe that each member of the family can also access the security footage on their mobile phones.'

'Right.' I nodded. This news was slightly unnerving, as it appeared that I could now be watched by a fair few people whenever they felt like it. Not that I was doing anything remotely interesting, just reading and writing a few notes. But still... 'I see. Er, break-in?'

'Yes,' Mr Brentwood said. 'It was all very strange. I was on duty myself that night. The burglar – whoever it was – chose to gain entry to the castle by climbing up an old iron drainpipe and letting themselves in through a window on the second floor. The odd thing was that the window wasn't broken; the police think that it had been left on the latch. It was such a specific choice of entry that we all believe that the intruder must have had inside knowledge, must have known that the window in question would be left open that night. Which of course then leads on to the natural and very uncomfortable conclusion that it may have been one of the staff. It would hardly have been a family member, as they all have access to the castle at all times. But then so do members of staff. So why the break-in? It just doesn't make sense, and we've never got to the bottom of it.'

I shook my head.

'How awful,' I said. 'What did the thief take?'

'Well, here the tale gets even stranger,' Mr Brentwood said.

'The person made their way – quite confidently it seems – to the Upper Library where you are working now. Nothing else of value in the castle was taken, but when the night guard found the burglar during his patrol, the library was in a state of chaos. Papers everywhere, boxes and files all over the floor.'

'So did the guard catch them?' I said.

'Unfortunately not,' Mr Brentwood said. 'Whoever the person was had the foresight to bring some sort of weapon with them, and poor Terry reports that before he could grab them, they hit him over the head and he collapsed. He wasn't quite rendered unconscious, more stunned, but he was unable to stop the person from escaping. It seems that they left the castle in the same manner that they arrived – through the second-floor window. The police conducted a thorough investigation afterwards, looked into Terry's life – much to the poor man's embarrassment – and trawled through all the CCTV that we had fitted at the time. But hardly anything of use was found, just a grainy image of the person making their way through one section of the grounds, but they were too far away to identify. Which makes it more likely that they had inside knowledge of how the castle was run at the time, as they managed to avoid being caught by most of the cameras that were set up at that point. And the window that they broke in through only leads to a tiny box room that wasn't alarmed at that point in time. Terry, of course, was completely cleared of any involvement.'

'Blimey,' I said, my head reeling with all this information. It was awful to think that the thief had made straight for the room I was working in. Quite unnerving. What could they have possibly been after in there? It was just full of documents and books, not exactly your typical treasure trove. 'So what did they get away with?'

'Ah.' Mr Brentwood shifted his position, suddenly looking a

bit uncomfortable. 'Now, Miss Haythorpe, you must understand that because of the wealth of private documents in that library, the cataloguing of them is still unfinished. Archibald Trengrouse made fine steps in putting them all in order, but when he died no other family member had the time or wherewithal to carry on his work. So in short, we're still unsure what the burglar took, if anything. The only thing that I do know is they created such a mess it took Mrs Taylor and I the best part of a week to tidy the room up again. We didn't find anything to be missing, but then as I said, it's so very hard to tell when we weren't sure what was there in the first place. No inventory exists that charts each document, you see. And while I've asked the family several times if they'd like me to make a list of each paper and book in there, they've declined every time. And I'm sure they have very good reasons for doing so,' he added quickly.

'Wow,' I said. 'The whole break-in does sound very strange. It doesn't seem to make sense. Because like you said, if it was a member of staff or even a family member who wanted to go through the library, they all have access to it anyway. Unless they leaked some information to one of their friends... And I wonder what it was that the burglar was after?'

'Your guess is as good as mine, Miss Haythorpe,' Mr Brentwood said, turning back to a giant rack of wines. 'But no need to worry about the cameras. They are just there for security, and I can guarantee that no one is snooping around watching you. Now if you'll excuse me, I must get on.'

As I walked back up the stone steps towards daylight, my mind was racing. A burglary in the very library that I was working in? It was just so strange. What on earth could the person have been after? And who were they?

'Aha,' a man's voice said as I reached the top step. 'There she is. We thought you'd disappeared, Grace. We've been looking everywhere for you.'

I turned to find Howard standing there, grinning at me. Next to him was an icily beautiful, stick-thin woman, who was staring at me in a detached and unamused way.

'Grace,' Howard said. 'Let me introduce you to my mother, Sukie.'

Chapter Seven

'Er, hi,' I said, sticking out my hand towards the woman. This was yet another strange turn of events. Why on earth would Howard want to introduce me to his mum? I was just a temporary member of staff. Something about it felt weird. 'So nice to meet you, Sukie.' Short for Susannah, I thought. I'd read a bit about Howard's parents before my arrival.

As her son looked at her, Sukie's face snapped into a well-practised but not altogether genuine – it seemed to me – beam.

'Grace, how wonderful to have you here at Godwyne with us.' Sukie took my hand and shook it. 'I hear you're an author?'

'Ah, yes,' I said, trying not to let my surprise at this encounter show on my face. 'I write non-fiction historical books, all based in the UK. I'm here to write one about the social scene in England in the 1900s.'

Hobnob the cat, I noticed, arrived several metres away from us, then sat down to observe the proceedings, her huge eyes unblinking.

'I read the one you wrote about Didecote Vicarage,' Howard said. 'Very good, I thought.'

'Wow, er, thank you,' I said. I hadn't been expecting that.

Hadn't presumed that anyone at the castle would have heard of me at all.

'What a splendid occupation,' Sukie said. 'I'm sure you'll find some rich material in the libraries at Godwyne. Especially about Cordelia; she and Archie caused something of a buzz in London during their time, I'm told.'

I nodded.

'And,' Sukie went on, 'Howard tells me that you're a distant relation of ours?' I opened my mouth, but nothing came out. Now this was a real shock. How on earth did Howard know that? It was such a small, trivial bit of information considering how far removed I was from the current family.

'Well,' I said, trying to regain my composure. 'I-I-'

'My wife, Mimi, loves genealogy,' Howard said. 'She's been on almost every ancestry site in existence, I think. When she heard that you were coming here, she said your name sounded familiar, and after a few checks she found you on a site called Our Heritage. She'd linked it with her page somehow. Sound familiar?'

'Ah, yes,' I said. 'Yes, I've made my own family tree on Our Heritage. Quite a few years ago now. Gosh, how lovely of Mimi to remember my name.'

I explained to them how the old family legend that we were somehow related to the Trengrouses from Godwyne Castle had been passed down through my mother's side of the family.

'Mimi wasn't sure exactly how we're related,' Howard explained. 'She just said she found your connection when searching up the family name, but that there's no completed family tree showing where you fit in.'

'No.' I shook my head. *God, I hope they didn't think I was some interloper who'd just made up some sort of grandiose connection with them for fun.* 'I haven't been able to track down the exact connection myself. I just put the name Trengrouse into my tree as a marker. But my mother was adamant that there's a link between us somehow. It probably goes back hundreds of years, or something.'

'I think it's delightful news,' Sukie said. But her eyes remained hard. 'And as a relation – no matter how distant – I insist that you join us for dinner tonight, Grace. It will be a chance for us all to get to know you better.'

'Well, if you're sure,' I said. 'I don't want to put you to any trouble.'

'Nonsense, I'll let cook know,' Sukie said as she turned away. 'Seven o'clock in the Lavender Dining Room.'

'See you there,' Howard said with a grin, before he turned to follow his mother.

'Right, see you then,' I said, watching them go. *Dinner? With the Trengrouse family?* My thoughts were spinning. I looked down at Hobnob, who was now purring round my ankles. So much had happened in one day, it was hard to take it all in. Howard had not only read one of my books, but the whole family seemed to know that I was a distant relation of theirs. It was unnerving, but also rather exciting. Not to mention everything else that had happened; the strange behaviour of Will, Alexandra's mysterious summons, and the discovery of the break-in. Then another thought struck me. *What on earth was I going to wear to dinner?* I'd only brought work clothes with me. It hadn't even crossed my mind that I'd ever be dining with the family. I'd never sat down to eat with any of the other families I'd written about before. *Right*, I decided. The research could wait for now. I needed to get my bags out of my car, find someone who could show me to my bedroom, and trawl through my clothes until I found a suitable outfit...

Chapter Eight

'Thank you, Mr Brentwood,' I said, as he nodded and retreated back into the corridor. I stared round my new bedroom. After my unexpected meeting with Howard and Sukie, I'd had to go back down to the cellars and accost the castle manager once more, asking him to show me where I'd be sleeping during my time at Godwyne. He'd only showed the slightest vexation on his face at yet another interruption, and had quickly gone and got a set of keys, and then shown me up to the top floor. It was where all the staff had rooms, he told me. It was a small but comfortable-looking space, perhaps a servant's room back in the old days. I imagined how it would have looked then; probably with bare floorboards and a narrow iron bed. It was much more comfortable now, with a carpet, bed 'with mattress topper', as Mr Brentwood had said, and a wardrobe and small chest of drawers.

The view from the window was definitely the best thing about my new living space, and I gazed out over the valley below, and the rolling hills beyond, realising that the view was pretty much the same as it would have been hundreds of years ago – bar the factory chimneys I could see in the distance. Once upon a time, the Trengrouse family would have owned all the land around the castle as far as the eye could see. I had no idea how much was still part of the estate, and which bits they'd had to sell off, but it was a relief to see the Cornish countryside around the castle remain so unspoilt. I realised that I could also see the odd bit of traffic trundling along a road some way off, but if you ignored that and the factory chimneys you could imagine that you were seeing the same view as those in the castle would have two hundred years ago.

My phone – lying on top of the bed – bleeped into life.

'Grace?' My sister's voice said as I pressed the green call button. 'Are you free to talk for a moment?'

'Hi, Penny, yes of course,' I said. 'What's up?'

'It's Gabby,' Penny said. 'She's not in a good way at the moment, and I'm exhausted. Neither of us have got much sleep for the last few nights, and I just needed to have a moan to you about it. Nothing too important.'

'Oh, you poor thing,' I said, feeling my stomach tighten as it did every time that I heard my niece was going through a bad patch. 'How's Gabby doing?'

'She's got another chest infection,' my sister said, and I could hear the emotion in her voice. Chest infections were common among cystic fibrosis sufferers and each one was worrying, as they made it all the more difficult for the person to breathe. 'The doctor has seen her and says she can stay at home for now. But it's so hard to watch her go through this, Grace.'

'I know,' I said, as my sister broke into sobs at the other end of the phone. 'I know it is, Pen, and you're doing such a fabulous job with Gabby. You're so strong, you're her rock.'

'No, I'm not doing a good job,' Penny said, catching her breath. 'I'm tired, I'm snappy and I feel like I'm coming to my wits' end. I just want her to get better enough to lead some sort of fulfilling life, do you know what I mean? We seem to have been stuck at home for ages now, just going round in circles. If only I could get her to America for that treatment...'

'I'm going to help you with that all I can,' I said, trying to soothe my distraught sister. I felt so useless and helpless when Gabby was ill; I desperately wanted to conjure up a magic cure for her but there just wasn't one. Her best chance was the new triple combination therapy in the US, we just needed to amass the funds to get Gabby there. It was too painful, listening to Penny's words, and I wished I was there with her so I could give her a huge hug. 'Listen, I'm going to work really hard on my new book, and hopefully I'll get a big advance...'

We chatted on for a while, and slowly I heard Penny's sobs subside and her breathing return to normal. It was worrying enough being Gabby's aunt, but for my sister it must be torture, watching her beloved daughter struggle to breathe so much.

'She's waking up from her nap,' Penny said, and I could hear Gabby's voice in the background, calling out for her mum. 'I better go.'

We said our goodbyes and I put the phone down, full of even stronger resolve about my purpose at the castle. It didn't matter how many bloody mysterious things happened at Godwyne; I was there for one reason only, and that was to start writing my best book yet. It was beyond important that we raised enough money to get Gabby over to America for treatment. Once I had the synopsis and first three chapters done, I could send it off to my agent, Daiyu, who could then start approaching publishers with it. And I fully trusted her when she said she'd get the best deal possible for me. She always did, and we'd known each other for long enough to know that both of us would keep to our promises.

I emptied the contents of my suitcase out onto the bed, and picked through them. I'd brought a fairly uninspired collection of clothes to Godwyne, mainly because I didn't think I'd need to ever dress up while I was there. I'd gone for comfort and convenience over style, with two pairs of jeans, a skirt and tights, a couple of jumpers, a shirt and T-shirt, as well as the necessary underwear and night clothes. No flashy dresses, no interesting jewellery, all that was still back in my London apartment. But then it didn't really matter what I wore to dinner, I realised. Because after all, I wasn't there to impress the Trengrouses.

I'd momentarily had my head turned by the glamour and mystique of it all, but Penny's call had brought me back to what really mattered and to what I was doing there. Dinner, I thought, would be a good chance to extract as much information about Archie and Cordelia from the family, and to learn as much as I could about the Trengrouses in the 1900s. Then tomorrow, when I'd had a good sleep and felt much fresher, I'd return to the library and immerse myself in my work completely, and forget about all the odd occurrences that had taken place since my arrival at the castle...

Chapter Nine

I wandered slowly through the castle as I attempted to locate the whereabouts of the Lavender Dining Room, my head now fully back in work mode. Now that I'd been reminded of the first and foremost reason I was at the castle, I was in no rush to get to dinner. The idea of eating with the family was now more tiring than anything else. The long day of travelling, working, being accosted by the unfriendly Will and the mysterious Alexandra was catching up with me. I was mulling thoughts about the book and my research around, wondering how much I'd be able to get done in the library the next day. It was imperative that I found some good hooks to impress Daiyu with, some really meaty titbits that would hook potential readers in. With all the documents that I'd seen earlier, there must be quite a few interesting stories in there. I just had to find them...

I paused to gaze at the dour paintings I passed in a dim corridor, the old family portraits, the suits of armour, the hanging swords, and the assortment of odds and ends that the Trengrouses had collected over the years, and put into display cabinets. They certainly had a lot of memorabilia about long-gone generations. So unlike 'normal' people, who didn't have all of this history around them about their ancestors. The most my mum had about her older relatives were a few photos, and her mother's old sewing box.

As I rounded a corner and walked through yet another sternly decorated room, a large map hanging over a fireplace caught my eye. Wandering closer, I saw that it was another depiction of Godwyne – similar to the one in the staff dining room – but this time including the castle as well as the grounds. It must have been an old piece of art, because it seemed to include the original estate boundaries, before much of the land round the edges was sold off to housing development companies. *Wow,* I thought, staring at the expansive design. *This place is huge. It must be worth millions. Billions, perhaps. The family must be one of the wealthiest in Britain, lucky things.*

I gazed at all the features that were set around the grounds, realising I'd only seen a fraction of what the estate held so far. There were so many outbuildings, as well as different stable blocks, the old icehouse, monastery ruins, statues, fountains, different gardens, a wild meadow, copses, woods and orchards – not to mention the giant castle sitting in the middle of it all. I'd only seen a small part of its interior so far. What would I find out about the place over the coming days? Would I come to realise exactly where the family lived in the castle? Or would it all remain a mystery...

What must it be like to be brought up with all this privilege? I wondered, dragging my eyes away from the map and turning towards the door. By the looks of things, Will didn't seem one who would appreciate his lot in life, whereas his brother Howard was much more charming and friendly. He was more likely to grow to appreciate his station in life, I thought. To understand how fortunate he was. But based on the obvious conflict in their personalities, what on earth would the rest of the family be like? Well, I'd soon find out, I mused, as a delicious-smelling waft greeted my nose. Hopefully they would be as welcoming as Howard, but from Sukie's fleeting expression earlier I wasn't counting on it. I must be close to the dining room now. And more importantly, what would they be able to tell me about Archie and Cordelia? I was hoping that I could get conversation about those two flowing at dinner, one way or another...

Chapter Ten

'Pass the wine, will you?' Will said, his voice demanding, his eyes glaring at me. I did as he asked; I already knew that there would be no point in attempting to engage Will in conversation at all during my stay at Godwyne, or to be affronted by his arrogant and rude attitude. From what I'd observed, and from what the other staff had said at lunchtime, I got the impression that he was always belligerent and wasn't about to change his approach in the near future. I'd decided that I wasn't going to take his behaviour personally, but neither was I at all interested in trying to understand him or what made him tick either. He was someone to be endured throughout my stay, and that was all.

I found the other people sitting around the grand, oval table much more fascinating. Sukie sat at one end, an ice queen robed in a pale-blue, long-sleeved dress that complimented her eye colour perfectly. A large glass of red wine sat in front of her. It was the second I'd observed her drinking since my arrival in the room. At the other end sat her husband, Edward, heir to the Godwyne estate. He was tallish, had a strong face, and it was obvious from his fading gingery hair where his sons got their own colouring from. He was sporting a Rolex watch on his wrist, wearing an expensive-looking shirt and seemed somewhat out of sorts and distracted, not joining in with the general conversation, but preferring to concentrate on the contents of his plate. To my left sat Howard, and next to him was his pretty young wife, Mimi, who were both discussing their weekend plans with Sukie in a lively manner. On the other side, near to Sukie, perched old Alexandra, her wide-eyed stare fixated on me, and next to her – opposite me – was Will. There was one more place set next to him, but as yet no one had arrived to take it.

'Grace,' Sukie was saying, turning her gaze on to me. 'Have you dug up any scandalous titbits about the Trengrouses yet? Mr Brentwood said you've been working in the Upper Library today.' She wound her fingers round the stem of her wine glass and picked it up.

'Mummy, she's been here less than a day,' Howard said, turning towards me. 'Give the poor girl a chance.'

I smiled back at him, appreciating his friendliness. I was starting to get the feeling, from my brief encounters with her, that his mother – Sukie – had a very low opinion of me. Why, I didn't know. But I was here to conduct research, and this conversation, I realised, could be an ideal opening into digging for information about Archie and Cordelia.

'No, nothing yet,' I said to Sukie with a smile. 'I've only read a few of Archie's diary entries so far. I'm very interested in his wife, Cordelia, actually. Wasn't she a famous socialite, in her day?'

'Yes,' Sukie said, not returning my smile. 'Cordelia knew all the right people. The prime minister of the time came to her soirées quite regularly, I believe. My husband would be the best person to tell you more about her. Eddie?'

'Hmm, what's that?' Edward looked up.

'We're just talking about Cordelia, darling,' Sukie said. 'You know, Archie's wife. Grace, the writer and your long-lost relative, wants to know more about her.'

For the first time, Edward properly looked at me. I mean, really acknowledged who I was. He'd grunted at me when I'd arrived in the Lavender Dining Room, feeling a tad nervous, but I don't think he'd really taken in who I was and why I was there at that point.

'Long-lost relative, eh?' he said. His eyes were raking me over, and as I gazed into them I got the feeling that he was a shrewd and intelligent man. 'Mother or father's side?'

'Er, my mum's,' I said. 'Although I've yet to find out the exact connection.'

'There probably isn't one,' Will said loudly. 'She just wants a step up in the world, don't you, Grace?'

I could feel a hot blush of humiliation spread across my cheeks.

'No, not at all,' I mumbled. 'It's just an old family tale that's been passed down to my sister and I, that's all.'

'Don't take any notice of Will,' Mimi said, leaning forwards so that she could see me. 'He's always beastly to everyone. He was definitely last in the queue when the manners were being handed out.'

Howard nodded, but Sukie and Edward, I noticed, didn't say anything. Either they were too used to their son's rudeness to notice it anymore, I thought, or they privately agreed with what he was saying.

'She's a Trengrouse all right,' old Alexandra said, pointing at me. 'She's...'

'Yes, that's enough, Mother,' Edward said sharply. 'Oh look, Cook's bringing another course in.'

At that point, just as Mary – who clearly had her work cut out – was dragging a heavily laden trolley through the door, a young girl with long russet curls sashayed past her and sat down at the empty chair. She looked no more than eighteen or nineteen. *She must be the boy's cousin,* I thought. *The 'airhead' that Mary had told me about at lunch.*

'Helena,' Sukie said, turning her stare onto the girl. 'Dinner starts at seven each evening. Edward? Tell her.'

Helena barely acknowledged Sukie's words, instead preferring to reach for the bottle of wine.

'Yes, quite, starts at seven,' Edward said, but I saw the mischievous wink that he gave his niece as she poured a steady stream of red into a glass. Hadn't Mary said that Helena managed to get a constant stream of money out of her uncle? It was easy to see how, as he clearly doted on the young girl. Perhaps, I wondered, because he'd never had any daughters of his own. Sukie, however, was clearly not quite so keen.

'Grace, meet my cousin, Helena,' Howard said. 'Helena, Grace is a writer. And a distant relation of ours.'

'How simply super,' Helena said, not looking in the slightest bit interested. She drained away half her glass in one go.

'Yes, one who's probably heard about what Archie buried in the grounds,' Will said. 'And wants to find the inheritance for herself.'

There was a hush at the table. Then Sukie, Howard and Mimi began talking all at once about three different things, all of them seemingly wanting to distract the attention from Will's words. But this information was the first worthwhile thing that I'd heard Will say all day.

'What did Archie bury in the grounds?' I said innocently, picking up my glass. I spoke quite loudly, in order to be heard over the distraction chattering that was going on. After I'd spoken, the table fell quiet again. Everyone, I noticed, was now staring at me.

'Well,' Edward said. 'If you're a relative of ours, Grace, as my mother apparently believes you are, then you deserve to be told. But please bear in mind that what I'm about to tell you isn't necessarily fact. It's an old family legend that's been handed down through the generations. And it's one that's had us all intrigued for years.'

I nodded, and waited for him to continue.

'Old Archie,' Edward went on, 'was a man with a fine mind. One of his great passions in life was archaeology, and he spent many years excavating the chapels on the estate, sometimes finding some rare artefacts that monks from previous centuries had buried.'

I nodded again.

'In fact, he was more interested in that than in anything else,' Edward went on. 'Especially as his children grew up and wanted to gamble and socialise as much as their mother did. One day, due to the constant arguing that was going on among his relatives about who was going to inherit what after he died, Archie – so the story goes – got so sick of all this backbiting and greed, that he decided to bury the priceless jewels that had been in the family since the time of William the Conqueror. It was with them, you see, that the main part of the inheritance – other than the bricks and mortar of Godwyne Estate – lay. And old Archie decided that he didn't particularly want to leave the jewels to any of his relatives. I think it was his way of punishing them for wasting their lives and his money. His wife Cordelia, so he thought, was ruining them with her constant socialising; never leaving him with enough funds to make the necessary repairs to Godwyne that Archie was aware needed doing. His children only seemed to have one thing on their minds, and that was to persuade him to leave each one of them the jewels. But he thought the whole lot of them shallow and vice-ridden, and he suspected, probably quite rightly, that if he left the treasure to any one of them, they would ruthlessly squander the lot and it would leave the family.'

'Which it probably would have,' Howard said, with a mock grimace.

'So rather than dig things up, as he did on his archaeological excursions,' Edward went on. 'Archie decided to bury something instead. He put the jewels somewhere in Godwyne's grounds. And each generation of Trengrouses have been looking for them ever since. At the time he did this, Archie knew that his health was ailing, and that he would probably die before any of the others, which in fact he did. But on his deathbed, he apparently told his wife that whoever deserved the jewels most would be the one to eventually find them. But as yet, no one has.'

I hung off each of Edward's words, enthralled to hear this story. It certainly explained Will and Sukie's animosity towards me; they must think that I was just a fortune hunter, come to do my best to find the priceless jewels. But although I'd read about the hidden treasure in old newspaper articles, I'd been prepared for it to just be a slice of fascinating family folklore, with nothing to it. But I didn't want to let on that I'd already heard of it, Will already thought I was a gold digger and I didn't want to give him any more ammunition. As it was, I couldn't even prove that I was a part of the Trengrouse tribe, even very distantly. All I had to go on was the tale handed down in my own family. I didn't want any of them thinking I was interested in getting my hands on the treasure, which of course, was a ludicrous idea. But it certainly gave me much to think about in terms of the book that I was writing. It was a key part of Archie and Cordelia's backstory that I may never have found recorded in the notes in the Upper Library. And it certainly gave me more of a definite hook with which to centre my book around.

I wasn't planning to betray the trust that Edward had placed in me by telling me this old family legend, but what he'd said certainly explained why Archie had mentioned the state of the house so much in the diary entries I'd read so far. Perhaps it would be possible for me to extract a fuller picture of Archie and Cordelia's disagreements, so that my book could not just be about the social scene in the 1900s, but also depict an intimate portrait of husband and wife who were at odds when it came to keeping up appearances versus the reality of the hardships to do with maintaining such a large estate...

Mary, who'd been listening to all this and had obviously heard it all before as she didn't show the slightest bit of interest, began placing plates in front of everyone. She then doled out the pudding, which was Eton Mess, pushed the trolley into a corner, and left the room.

The meal went on without interruption after that. After we'd finished, I said my goodbyes, thanked the family for their kind hospitality, and made my excuses to leave, saying – quite truthfully – that I was very tired after such a busy day.

I'd made my way out of the Lavender Dining Room, down the corridor and round the corner, when I heard footsteps behind me.

'Wait right there,' the unmistakable tones of Alexandra said. 'I have something extremely important that I need to tell you.'

Chapter Eleven

I stopped, and waited for her to catch up with me. She walked slowly, hobbling a little, but each stride contained great purpose. When she finally reached my side, I was glad to see that we were hidden from anyone else's view. I didn't particularly want any of the family members to see us talking, because while they seemed to think that 'Granny' was a few eggs short of a batch – which she might be – it felt important that I wasn't seen having secret conversations with anyone. There was enough animosity and mistrust towards me at present from at least two of the Trengrouses, and I certainly didn't want to fan the flames of any of that.

'How can I help you, Alexandra?' I said.

'It's not how you can help me,' she said. 'It's a matter of how I can help you, Grace.'

'What do you mean?' I said.

'I know you are a relative of mine,' she said. 'I have proof.'

I smiled.

'That's fantastic news, Alexandra,' I said. 'I've always wanted to know how I'm related to the Trengrouses. Don't tell me, am I a fifteenth cousin seven times removed?'

Alexandra shook her head, causing her long white hair to float around wispily.

'No,' she said. 'You are much closer than that. Much, much closer.'

I could feel my brow crinkling as I took in her words.

'In what way?' I said. 'Surely that's impossible, or there would be clear links to me on the official family trees.'

'Not if there was a cover-up,' Alexandra said, moving her face even closer to mine. 'There's not one selfish blighter sitting at that table that would give you this information, Grace, even if they knew what I'm about to tell you, which I'm not sure they do. Because they're as money grabbing and desperate as Archie Trengrouse's own immediate family. But the fact is, you're in line for that inheritance, for those buried jewels, as much as Edward, Howard, Will and the rest of them are.'

I blinked. *Oh God*, I thought. *She is mad after all...*

'Right,' I said. 'What do you mean?'

'Listen to me very carefully,' Alexandra said. 'Archie had a daughter, Beatrice, who had a baby with her husband when they were very young. Now because Beatrice was the black sheep of the family and had been shunned by her mother and other siblings after Archie died, the family concocted a cover-up so that the inheritance, if it was ever found, would never go to Beatrice's son, Jacob.'

'But why would they do that?' I said.

'Because he had epilepsy,' Alexandra said, her voice now a hiss. 'And in those days that sort of condition was looked upon as madness. Many children who suffered from it ended up in lunatic asylums, or with people saying that they were possessed by the devil. Society could be very cruel then. Cordelia wanted the inheritance to go to her favoured grandchild, her daughter Ottilie's son, Francis. She wanted him to be the one who ended up inheriting Godwyne and finding the jewels. The other two daughters didn't have children, of course. Lettie entered a convent and Alice never married. Archie never had an heir himself, which is why his wife took over and interfered so much. Cordelia thought that bad genes would be spread if Jacob bred and carried on the family name. Godwyne did end up going to Francis, but none of them ever found those jewels.'

'So what you're saying,' I said slowly, 'is that I'm related to Beatrice and Jacob somehow?'

'Yes,' Alexandra said. 'That's exactly what I'm telling you, Grace. Archie wasn't just my great grandfather. He was also your great, great, great grandfather. You're directly related to him, just as all the other idiots who were at dinner are. Francis was my father, and Ottilie my grandmother. Beatrice was your great, great grandmother, and Jacob was your great grandfather. But both Beatrice and Jacob were shuffled off somewhere obscure with a big payout, and the family lines were deliberately obscured after that.'

'That's awful,' I said.

'Yes it is.' Alexandra's clear eyes stared at me. 'The family put the story about that Jacob had been conceived out of wedlock and was therefore illegitimate, but that was a load of tosh. He was very much legitimate. Cordelia wanted to stamp out any trace of Jacob altogether, you see. She made Beatrice promise that she'd never tell Jacob that he was related to the Trengrouses, and I'm sure she had some awful hold over her daughter, because I'm pretty sure that Beatrice – or her husband John – never told Jacob the truth about his family. Perhaps the money they received every year was given on the condition that they kept to their end of the bargain. And by the time Cordelia died, the damage had been done. Beatrice died at a fairly young age, heartbroken after her husband had died at sea. I expect Jacob grew up rather confused about his roots. Either that, or Beatrice invented some sort of story to tell him, which – judging from the fact you knew you were somehow distantly related to the rest of us – I expect involved being very vaguely related to the Trengrouses at Godwyne Castle. Because at least that bit of information has been handed down in your family. And Jacob's surname was different. It wasn't Trengrouse, it was Stewart, after his father's.'

'But Jacob must have had children at some point,' I said.

'Yes, as far as I can gather he married twice and had four children in total,' Alexandra said. 'Three of them died, but one survived. And that must be your grandparent. Grandmother, to be precise.'

'Do you know what she was called?' I said, my voice now coming out no louder than a whisper. If what old Alexandra was saying was true, my whole world had just been turned upside down and inside out.

'I believe that it was Rosalind, which was shortened to...'

'Rosie,' I said. 'That was my grandma's name.' My thoughts were reeling now. It was all too much to take in. 'My mum's told me all about her. I never met her though...'

I paused.

'Hang on,' I said. 'My grandma's father wasn't called Jacob. Mum always told us that his name was...'

'James?' Alexandra said. And then she smiled at my flabbergasted nodding. 'Yes,' she went on, 'it's an old Trengrouse family tradition for the boy's middle name to be James. Perhaps Jacob was never even told his first name. The whole thing was so sad, and so unnecessary.'

'But if Jacob was shuffled off and lied to, then doesn't that make him obsolete in terms of family history?' I said. 'I mean, even if I am directly related to him, I'm sure that no one in the family would accept my status as being directly related to Archie.'

'You're wrong there,' Alexandra said. A look of anger

clouded her features. 'What was done to Beatrice and her son was barbaric. There's nothing wrong with a child just because they have epilepsy, and we all know that today. Jacob was the rightful heir, as he was born before Francis. Beatrice was the oldest child. And Jacob wasn't illegitimate, he was perfectly legal, and I have the documentation to prove it. I have Beatrice's wedding certificate, and I have Jacob's birth certificate in my room. Which is why I was trying so desperately to get you to come and see me, so that I could give them to you. They belong to you, Grace. Although if any of the others know that I have them, they'll destroy them without a thought. Mark my words. They don't want any other rightful claimants to Godwyne popping up at this stage.'

'What do you mean?' I said. I was feeling a bit dizzy now.

'I mean that everyone here has their own deep, dark secrets, my dear,' Alexandra said. 'Everyone has reasons for wanting to find the money. I know they're my own relations, but none of them care a jot about me. Edward can't wait till I'm dead so that he can do what he wants with the castle, and they all tell anyone who'll listen that I'm as mad as a bag of monkeys. But I'm not, I know exactly what I'm talking about.'

'W-w-where did you find the marriage and birth certificates?' I said.

'Before my eyesight went, I was as interested in genealogy as young Mimi is,' Alexandra said. 'But in those days there was no internet, I had to do it all by hand. In the exact room that you're working in now, the Upper Library. I read through as many papers as I could, and I found a trail left by Archie that pointed to what had happened to Beatrice. Cordelia may have never loved her, but Archie did. I think he was distraught at what happened to her and Jacob, but for some reason it seems that he could never stand up to his wife. She always seemed to have the upper hand in everything. I think hiding the family jewels was his last act of defiance against her. That, and preserving documentation relating to his eldest daughter and Jacob. You'll find it all in the library, if you look closely enough.'

'I see,' I said, exhaling.

'Come and see me during the night, my dear, and I'll give you the certificates,' Alexandra said. 'You need to have them for your own records, they will be the starting point for you to prove your very close connection to this godforsaken family. But be very, very careful. Everyone here might seem harmless, but I can assure you that most of them are as ruthless as a highwayman, and would do anything to guard the remaining wealth attached to Godwyne.'

I nodded, thanked her, and took her hands in mine. I had my own, very personal reason, for knowing that what Alexandra was saying was true. I'd been diagnosed with epilepsy as a child. And I knew that it could be a hereditary condition, passed down through genes, although my mother and father had never suffered from it. I only rarely told people now, as I'd outgrown the condition, as many children do. But the coincidence was too great. Jacob had had it, and so had I.

It was at that moment that I heard the footsteps running away in the corridor round the corner. I dashed to look, but all I caught was the sight of a door closing at the end of the passageway.

'Someone's been listening to us the whole time,' I said. A wave of nausea, caused by the implications of this, overtook me.

Chapter Twelve

As I opened the door to my room, I stopped. Was it my imagination, or had someone been in here while I was at dinner? My bag and belongings looked ruffled on the bed, and in different positions than I'd left them. Well, if a person had been snooping around, they wouldn't have found anything very interesting among my stuff. Just a laptop – which was still there – clothes, a phone charger, a few books and bits of stationery, and toiletries. Luckily I'd taken my handbag and phone with me to dinner, so I knew no one had been through those.

But, I thought, closing the door and clearing a space on the bed before flopping down onto it. Perhaps my nerves were just on high alert now, after the extraordinary truths Alexandra had just revealed to me. Maybe no one had been in my room, and I was just imagining the whole thing. Hearing the footsteps in the corridor after I'd finished chatting to Alexandra, and seeing the end door close had really freaked me out. I knew that I hadn't imagined *them*. There was no point trying to work out who it was that had overheard our conversation. All the Trengrouses – according to Alexandra – had deep, dark secrets and if any of them even suspected that I was in line for the inheritance, or in fact had more of a claim over it than them, if I really was descended from the rightful heir to the castle – Jacob – (who'd been so cruelly deposed all those years ago) then it didn't take much imagination to work out that they'd want to listen to any clandestine conversations that I had with other people.

There were so many dates and names, that it was hard to get my head around the whole thing in one go. So if I'd got this correct, Alexandra had been saying that Archie was her great grandfather, Ottilie her grandmother and Francis her father. And that Archie was my great, great, great grandfather, Beatrice my great, great grandmother, Jacob my great grandfather, and of course Rosie had been my grandma. My mum, Martha, had died never knowing this connection with the Trengrouses, which made me sad. It looked like Penny and I were the only living relatives on this line of the family, as Mum had been an only child, so we hadn't had any cousins.

While I'd felt genuine emotion from Alexandra, and had a hunch that she was telling me the truth – especially with the remarkable coincidence that both Jacob and I had suffered from epilepsy – I knew that in order to fully put weight on what she'd said, I needed to see the proof with my own eyes. Needed to go to her later that evening, and collect the marriage and birth certificates. Because they would give me a concrete place to start, the first stepping stone in being able to trace my ancestry directly back to Archie Trengrouse. I could contact Penny too, and ask if she'd kept any records that Mum had left us about the family; she'd always been more of a hoarder than me. I knew that I could also look online at genealogical websites and try and trace my roots that way, but I'd tried that before, and had come to a dead end.

I had a feeling that Cordelia would have tried to hide or destroy Jacob's birth certificate, and that somehow Archie had ended up with it and had looked after it for safekeeping. But that it had never been registered with any public agency; perhaps Cordelia had managed to muddy the waters as far as church records went so that no descendants would ever be able to trace themselves back to Jacob and the Trengrouses. Or maybe his birth certificate had been registered under a false name. There were so many possibilities. And I knew – from my previous research into aristocratic British families – how corrupt many of them were a hundred years ago, how several had interfered with documents and facts in order to bend certain outcomes of events to their own advantages. It certainly wasn't unthinkable or improbable that Cordelia had taken this course of action.

If I was directly related to Archie, and as much a part of the family as the rest of the people who'd sat round the table at dinner, then the implications were huge. And in the forefront of my mind, as I mulled this over, was my niece Gabby. If I was entitled to something – anything – financially, then I would be able to fly Gabby and Penny over to America, as well as pay for the desperately needed triple combination therapy, which would give my niece a chance at living the healthiest and best life possible. And the thought that I might be able to do this sooner rather than later – especially as Gabby was ill again – if I could just prove my place in the family, was thrilling. Perhaps there was a trust fund that living relatives were entitled to? I had no idea, but Edward, Sukie and the rest of them must get their money from somewhere.

A day ago, this thought would never even have entered my head. Even in my most crazy dreams, I could have never conjured up the circumstances that I now found myself in. But now I felt compelled, with every fibre of my body, to find out the truth about my place in the family. And I couldn't let myself fully believe in it until I'd seen concrete evidence with my own eyes.

But first, I thought, *before I go and visit Alexandra later, I need to get some sleep.* A deep exhaustion was now replacing the adrenaline, excitement and apprehension that I'd been feeling since my meeting with the old lady. My going to her room later was now not in question. Yes, I was worried that if anyone saw me, my credibility as a guest at Godwyne would be severely tarnished, unless I could think up an amazing excuse as to why I was tiptoeing round the castle in the dead of night. But finding out about the truth of my lineage had trumped all that, it was now even more important than my reputation. What had Alexandra said earlier when I'd seen her at lunchtime? 'Follow the white roses,' to find her bedroom. I had no idea what that meant, but I intended to work it out after I'd had a nap. I knew that a clearer head was required for what lay ahead and at that moment my head was full of thick fuzz.

I reached for my phone, set the alarm for 1.30am – which I figured was late enough to ensure that most people – if not everyone – would be in their rooms, hopefully asleep. Then I put my laptop on the dressing table and swept the rest of my belongings onto the floor, stretched out on the bed, and fell into a deep sleep.

Only to be woken up an hour later, by that piercing shriek. The one that I'll never, ever be able to forget...

Chapter Thirteen

I sat bolt upright, and waited. It took me a few seconds to work out exactly where I was. Had I imagined the scream? Had I dreamt it? I wondered.

No, there it was again. Now I could hear running footsteps, and loud, urgent voices speaking. Then I heard footsteps crunching on the gravel outside my window. More voices. What the hell was going on? What had happened?

It sounded like more people were gathering outside. Someone was sobbing. My bedroom was now illuminated by all the security lights that the outdoor activity had triggered. It was spooky, it felt almost like daylight. Surreal and scary.

I got out of bed, opened the window and peered down.

Alexandra was lying on the ground below, and by the twist of her neck I realised that there was no possibility she could be alive. Her eyes were open, staring, the expression on her face was one of shock. Her limbs were bent at unnatural angles, her white hair splayed out around her head like a halo.

My hands went to my mouth, as a wave of horror overtook me. How could this be? It was like a horror film. But it was real life. I couldn't take it in. What the hell had happened to her? I'd just been speaking to her, only a few hours previously. The pose she was in suggested that she'd fallen quite a long way from somewhere in the building. Or had she been pushed? The thought made me shake. How the fuck did a nice old lady end up flat on her back – clearly dead – on gravel in the middle of the night?

Mimi, bending over her, was the one sobbing. I could tell that from the way her body was shuddering. Howard was down there too, his arm round his wife's waist. He had his mobile phone in the other hand. Will was standing there, separate from the other two, and for once he was quiet. Mr Brentwood was pacing nearby, one hand on his forehead, the other clutching his phone to his ear. Mrs Taylor arrived and bent down to tend to Alexandra, opposite Mimi. I could see Edward and Sukie walking towards them. Helena was the only absent family member. And there was no sign of Mary, Zara or Jesse. Maybe they didn't sleep on site, although I was pretty sure that Mr Brentwood had told me that everyone who worked for Godwyne lived in the castle.

I should go down, I thought. *See if there's anything I can do to help.*

But I was frozen to the spot, unable to stop staring at the grotesque scene that was playing out below me. Unable to tear my eyes away from Alexandra, who only hours before had imparted such life-changing information to me. What was adding to the sickening dreadfulness of the whole thing, was the realisation that there may well be a connection between someone listening to what Alexandra had been telling me, and her subsequent death a few hours later. My alarm hadn't gone off yet, so it couldn't even be 1.30am yet.

I reached over, grabbed my phone and stared at it. 11.54pm.

A noise in the corridor outside my room made me jump. A

new layer of fear pervaded my brain. Could someone be coming for me now? So soon, after they'd killed Alexandra?

I directed my body, which was working jerkily now, towards the door. I took a deep breath, opened the door and stepped out into the dimly lit corridor.

And bumped straight into a tallish man who put his arms out to grab me.

My mouth opened and I screamed as loudly as I could.

Chapter Fourteen

'Get off me,' I shouted, pushing the man away. 'Leave me alone. Let me get past.'

'Hey,' the man said. His voice was calm and sounded surprisingly familiar. 'Don't worry, Grace. I'm not here to hurt you. It's me, Jesse. The groundsman. We met earlier, remember?'

'Oh.' I took a step away from him. Yes of course it was Jesse. I could see that now, could see his anxious eyes peering at me, his muscly arms outstretched as though to give me a hug. 'What are you doing up here?'

'I'm also a part-time night guard here at the castle,' Jesse said, lowering his arms. 'Terry's been off sick a lot since the break-in last year. After he found Alexandra, Howard phoned me and asked me to come and check on you and Helena, make sure you're both okay. Helena's not in her room, she must have gone out again, she's always doing that. Sorry, I didn't mean to make you jump.'

I nodded. This all made sense.

'I saw poor Alexandra out of my window,' I said, feeling very choked up. 'She's dead, isn't she?'

Jesse nodded.

'Looks like her neck's broken. Mr Brentwood's called an ambulance,' he said. 'I'm so sorry that this is happening on your first night here at Godwyne Castle, Grace. Things round here are usually so different. Nothing ever happens.'

Sirens pierced the air outside and I could hear wheels crunching over the gravel.

'I should go down there,' I said. 'See if there's anything I can do to help.'

Jesse nodded.

'I'll come with you,' he said.

Once we were outside with everybody else, things turned into a surreal blur. The sight of poor, dead Alexandra on the ground, stressed voices, crying, paramedics getting out of their ambulance, watching Alexandra being gently laid onto a stretcher. People pointing upwards, me following their gazes, to see an open, second-storey window – a white curtain billowing out of it like a ghost. It was overwhelming, intense and utterly awful.

Edward climbed into the ambulance to travel to the hospital with his mother, his face ashen. Sukie made arrangements to travel behind them with Mimi and Howard. Will disappeared off somewhere. At some point Zara the accountant and Mary the cook arrived, with Zara explaining that the noise from the siren had cut through her earplugs. Both were as shocked as the rest of us had been when they were told the news.

Jesse asked if everyone left would like to come back to his cottage for a drink.

'We've all had a shock,' he was saying. 'I know that I certainly won't be able to get much sleep now.'

Mr Brentwood and Mrs Taylor politely declined, and made their way back towards the castle. I also thanked him for his kind offer, but said I better get back to my room and try and sleep, as I had a lot of work to do in the morning. In reality, I just wanted to be alone, wanted to try and get my head around the horrendous event that had just occurred, and the awful implications of it. In the end, it was just Zara and Mary who went off with Jesse.

I wandered slowly back towards what I thought was the side door that Jesse and I had come out of earlier. In the rush of making our way downstairs, I hadn't taken in where we were going, or the route we'd taken. There were so many doors to the castle, and once inside there seemed to be so many routes to each place and floor. I figured that if I just did my best and tried to get up to the top floor, I'd get back to my room somehow.

It was eerie, entering the cold, faintly lit castle. The family – sensibly – seemed to like to save electricity during the night, and only very dull orangey lights – spaced quite far apart – illuminated each space. Everything in there suddenly seemed much more foreboding than it did in the daylight. The suits of armour, propped upright to the sides of the corridor, seemed alive. The darkened corridors seemed to hold a myriad of fearful possibilities. Each closed door taunted me as I walked past, threatening to open and reveal a scene of horror inside.

Get a grip, Grace, I told myself. *For goodness' sake, there's no one around but you now.*

That's when I heard the hushed voices. I stopped and held my breath. I was at the end of a corridor, and had found a side set of stairs that I was about to ascend. But instead, I worked out which room the voices were coming from, and listened intently, taking a small step towards it.

'Are you sure?' It was Mr Brentwood's voice. 'I mean, this is all quite worrying, Margaret.'

'Yes, yes, I'm quite sure of what I heard.' Mrs Taylor sounded agitated. 'Like I said, I was just on my way up to my room, after dinner had been cleared away and I'd set the

Lavender Dining Room right again. I heard two people talking, and I wasn't trying to overhear what they were saying, but I couldn't help it. One of them said, "It has to be done soon, do you understand?" Then I hurried away, it felt wrong to be listening. And then the next thing I know, poor Lady Trengrouse is found dead outside.'

Chapter Fifteen

'Hmm,' Mr Brentwood said. 'And did you recognise the voice?'

'I-I-I-, well, no,' Mrs Taylor said. Although she didn't sound very certain.

There was a pause.

'I think the best thing to do for the moment, Margaret,' Mr Brentwood said, 'is to keep this bit of information to ourselves. I'll try and do some investigating, and no doubt we'll have all sorts of people here at the castle tomorrow, trying to establish the cause of death. If we don't know who said those words, we can't understand the exact context behind them. For all we know, they were spoken quite innocently. And everyone here will be shaken up enough as it is; we don't want to go worrying them with any new developments unless we know for certain that what you heard has relevance to Lady Trengrouse's demise.'

I hurried away at that point, scaling the stairs in double-quick time. After getting lost twice, I eventually made my way back to my room, and threw myself down onto the bed.

Oh God, I thought. *What the hell is happening here? What kind of horrific mess have I walked into just by arriving at this castle?* My mind was whirring, my pulse racing. All I could think about was that earlier that evening, Alexandra had told me that I was directly related to Archie, and had even more right to any inheritance than the family who lived at the castle. Someone had overheard this conversation, then Mrs Taylor had heard a person saying 'It has to be done soon', and the next minute Alexandra is found dead on the ground. Could someone really have killed her on purpose? It was a horrific thought, because if it was true, it meant that someone I'd met since arriving at Godwyne was a murderer. And the only motive I could see behind such an action, was that this person knew that Alexandra had proof about me and my ancestry. Shit. Fuck. *What the hell should I do?* I mean, I was in fear for my own life now. Maybe everything was fine, and maybe Alexandra's death was an accident, and all the other factors could be innocently explained away. But on the other hand, maybe not. Maybe whoever was behind all this would be coming after me next.

I turned over, then turned over again. I was here to write a book good enough to garner a big advance so I could help send little Gabby for treatment in America. This thought was the one and only reason that I was considering staying on at the castle. I wasn't bothered about being part of the Trengrouse family; social climbing had never been my thing. But the tantalising possibility of gaining some easy money to give to my sister and niece had been too much to ignore.

But, I reasoned, I'd be no help to Penny and Gabby if someone finished me off, would I? No, the best thing to do would be to pack up early tomorrow morning, and go back home. I could reassess my situation, and quickly decide on another book to write. There were loads of stately homes and quirky rich families in Britain, it wouldn't be too hard to come up with a new book idea that had a strong hook, would it? The only problem with that, I realised, was that it took time to make introductions, time for the family to agree to me researching their ancestors, and more time to arrange travel and accommodation. And the one thing that Gabby didn't have on her side was time.

Urgh, this was too awful. I turned over again. Maybe I could look into taking out a large loan? Although I'd done that a year ago, and hadn't been offered one large enough to pay for the flights and the treatment. Although at this stage, anything would help and I might have better luck with it now...

Maybe I should just stay at Godwyne, I thought. *Just take my chances, keep myself to myself and get immersed in the research.* Once I had enough, I could go home and start writing the book in my apartment. An image of Alexandra dead and staring flashed through my mind. *No*, I decided. *If I'm going to help Penny and Gabby I need to be alive. And I'm not convinced that that would be a given, if I stay any longer at this castle. I've made up my mind. Tomorrow morning, I'm going to pack up my things and drive back to London. And that's that.*

Chapter Sixteen

I awoke from a fitful sleep to see daylight coming in through the curtains. A bird was tweeting a loud tune nearby. What was the time? I checked my phone. 7.26am. Time for me to pack up and leave.

It didn't take me long to get washed, dressed and then to throw my sparse belongings into my bag. I opened my bedroom door, with the plan to tiptoe all the way downstairs and out to my car. I didn't feel like explaining my departure to anyone; it wasn't exactly as though I could explain why I was terrified, as whoever I told would either think I was mad – claiming to be a direct descendant to Archie – or they would already know and be extremely unhappy about it. I'd send Mr Brentwood an email later, and say that I'd been called back to London on urgent business or something.

Just then, my phone – which was in my pocket – bleeped into life.

I withdrew it, and frowned when I saw the name flashing up. It was Penny. It was very unusual for her to be phoning me so early in the morning.

'Oh, Grace,' she said in a strangled voice when I answered. 'I'm so sorry to phone you like this, but I had to talk to someone.'

'What is it?' I said, closing the bedroom door again. 'Has something happened?'

'Yes,' Penny said, her voice becoming a wail. 'It's Gabby. She got taken into hospital last night. She's really poorly this time, Grace. I don't know what to do. I'm so scared.'

'Do you want me to come straight to you?' I said, an icy chill taking quick hold of my insides. 'Because I can drop everything here and drive straight over, Pen?'

'No, there's no point,' Penny said. 'They've put Gabs in isolation as they don't want any outside germs to get to her. I'm only allowed to see her for an hour each day apparently. You wouldn't be able to see her at all. Oh God, Grace, what am I going to do? I need to get her to America so badly. The drug that they would give her there would make her CFTR gene mutation function so much more effectively, it would pretty much make her better, Grace. Apparently the trials have consistently shown improvement in lung function and bad respiratory symptoms in patients, and both of those are what's currently making Gabby so poorly. She can barely breathe at the moment.'

'Right, don't worry. I'm going to get you the money you need,' I said. I was aware that these words were coming out of my mouth, and the promise that I was making my sister. I knew that I was taking a gamble by saying this, as with books and writing there were no guarantees. But I also knew that I was Penny's best and only option, and I was prepared to move heaven and earth to help her get Gabby the treatment that she needed so badly. 'I'm going to do it, okay? I'll get the money to you as soon as I can.'

'Oh, could you?' my sister said, exhaling. 'Oh God, Grace, that would be wonderful. It would save Gabby's life, I'm sure, if she could just get access to that treatment. I can't bear seeing her like this...'

I calmed my sister down, and made her promise to give me regular updates, and also to tell me if she needed me back in London.

When we finally said our goodbyes and rang off, I sat down on my bed and put my bag on the floor.

I wasn't going anywhere now, I realised. I was staying at Godwyne to write this bloody book, and to get to the bottom of my connection with the Trengrouses. Even if it meant risking my own life to do it. I was even going to go and search for the damn jewels that were allegedly buried in the grounds. Getting access to money would save my niece's life, and I was prepared to do whatever it took to help do this. And by the sounds of things, if poor Gabby was back in hospital – where she'd spent so much of her young life already – I would be working against the clock. Every second counted. Right. I had to get to work fast...

Chapter Seventeen

'Morning, Mary,' I said, passing the cook – who was wheeling a trolley laden with bacon, eggs, croissants and jugs of orange juice down the corridor. The castle layout – or at least some of it – was at last becoming familiar to me, and I realised that I was finding my way to the Upper Library much more easily that morning.

'Hello there, Grace,' Mary said. Then she leant in towards me. 'Have you heard the news?'

'Er, what news?' I said. I really wanted to be on my way, but I also didn't want to be rude. Mary had made me feel welcome at Godwyne, unlike some of the others. And as I was now determined to stay here and research the hell out of my next book, I needed to keep the nice members of staff onside.

'The family are already saying that poor Lady Trengrouse's death was an accident,' she said, her voice low.

'Really?' I said, my tone giving away more surprise than I intended. 'Are they sure? There has to be an investigation into it first, doesn't there, before any decisions like that are made?'

'Well, Zara overheard Mrs Taylor telling Mr Brentwood that almost all of the family members have told the police how much Lady Trengrouse used to wander around unaided recently,' Mary said. 'Put herself in a fair few spots of danger. Apparently they've been really worried about her over the last few years. I heard that Howard once found her on the main road, walking up towards the motorway. They showed the police her medical records, and if my sources are right, like I said, they are pretty sure that her death was an accident.'

'I see,' I said. It was really important that I didn't share my own private hunches with anyone, not even Mary. 'I have to say that I'm surprised that they've come to this conclusion so quickly.'

'Well, I don't think anything's been decided by the police officially yet,' Mary said. 'But if Lady Trengrouse was given to wandering, then it makes sense that she had a fall yesterday evening, doesn't it? If you ask me, the family should have been keeping a closer eye on her. Anyway, Hobnob finally turned up this morning. I was getting a bit worried about her – she scarpered last night during all the drama, and I couldn't call her in no matter how hard I tried. Never has liked bad energy, that one.'

After saying goodbye to Mary, I made my way to the library, pulled a desk into a corner where I was sure the video camera wouldn't be able to see me – as I didn't fancy being watched, either innocently or maliciously. Then I stopped for a second next to the old cabinet, crammed full with dusty objects. They were probably Archie's, I thought. They looked the type of things that had been dug up by someone who cared about archaeology. If things weren't so critical right now, I'd have taken the time to examine them. But I had more pressing things to do. I sat down, and opened my laptop.

That's when I saw it. The folded piece of paper.

I picked it up, spread it out, and began to read.

'My dear Grace,' the letter said, in large, wobbly

copperplate writing. 'I'm taking the precaution of writing to you directly. Do forgive the intrusion into your room, but I had to get word to you as soon as I could. So someone *had* been in my room yesterday, I *hadn't* been imagining things. I just wanted to say that if anything were to happen to me, anything at all, you must continue to dig deeper into the family documents yourself. Go to my bedroom, and collect what you can. Find the proof that you're entitled to the inheritance. And find the jewels. Follow Archie's trail. I tried, but in the end my eyesight failed me, I couldn't read the end of it. But I know it's all there. I would much rather it go to you than to any of the bloodsuckers that I share this castle with. I know you're a good person. Don't give up, Grace. You'll get there if you look hard enough.'

Underneath the paragraph was a signature, written in a shaky hand: Alexandra.

I sat back. Wow. So Alexandra herself had been aware enough to realise that something awful might happen to her. The idea that she'd fallen accidentally out of a high window – I now realised – was preposterous. She'd even felt the need to warn me in this way, and so quickly after I'd arrived at the castle. She'd known that her life was in danger, but still the brave woman risked everything by talking to me about what she knew. I now knew two things for sure: 1) that Alexandra had definitely been murdered. And 2) that I wasn't going to let her death be in vain. I already had a more than compelling, utterly urgent motive to write this book and learn the truth about my inheritance. But as I stared down at Alexandra's note, I realised that I wanted to honour her wishes, and to find out the truth for her, and for me.

If her death ended up being ruled an accident, as Mary had said, then what should I do with this note? I had absolutely no evidence – yet – that anything sinister had gone on; just my strong gut feeling and several conversations –

either my own, or overhead ones – which on their own, would mean nothing to a detective. Perhaps I should tell the police my hunch? Or would they just think I was mad, or worse still, start investigating me? Given everything that had happened, maybe the best thing was if I stayed out of it, and drew the least attention possible. After all, Gabby and Penny needed the money, and if I started making a fuss it would be even harder to write the book...

Hot anger boiled through my blood. What kind of wicked person would kill a lovely elderly lady just for inheritance? It made me sick to think about it. Well, I'd be on my guard twenty-four hours a day while I was at Godwyne. The killer could try their best with me, but I wasn't intending to let them get very far. I had more important things to do.

Right, I had to think clearly. I fired up the laptop, then went to browse the library's shelves. I no longer wanted to find out details about Cordelia's social life; I needed to find Archie's records that contained details of his ousted eldest daughter, Beatrice; the one that his wife Cordelia had so cruelly managed to disinherit. This was my new hook. The one I would write about, whether the family liked it or not...

The period I would be looking for would be later than the one I'd already delved into. Beatrice had still been a baby in 1900. I needed to establish the birth years of Archie's children, and go from there.

An hour later, I'd found out the dates that Archie's four daughters were born on. Ottilie – 1901, Lettie – 1903, and Alice – 1905. I knew – from my previous research about the family – that Beatrice was Archie's firstborn of four, a daughter who'd arrived in the world in 1899, when Archie was just twenty-one. I figured that with her epilepsy, things would never have gone well for Beatrice, poor thing, with her mother being as prejudiced as she sounded. But it sounded like life took a drastic turn for the worse when Beatrice married. She'd been a young wife, Alexandra had said. But how young did that mean?

I stared at the rows of files and boxes, wondering which one to try first. In the end I picked up a box labelled '1910 – 1912' and opened it. There were several documents on the top, and as I picked them up, I saw a diary underneath. I flicked it open, and saw – in now familiar writing – the name 'Archie Trengrouse' inscribed.

Sitting down again, I flipped the first page open. A photo fell out, and I knew at once that it was of Archie. As I stared into his eyes, I wondered what he must have been thinking at the time the photo was taken. He looked more careworn than in the image I'd seen of him as a younger man. More wrinkles round the eyes, less of a beaming smile. Perhaps money worries and the behaviour of his family members – not least his wife – had contributed to his ageing?

Moving the photo aside, I began to read.

> *April 1910. Cordy in London again, this time with Ottilie. She will be a debutante in seven years' time, and has most definitely inherited her mother's appetite for social events. Lettie is the scholar, Alice loves horses, but Beatrice is the one I worry about. It seems that nothing can compel Cordy to treat her with the same love and affection as she does the others. The good news is that poor Beatie hasn't had an episode for quite a while. Have managed to discourage the idea that she be sent away. For now, at least...*

I stopped reading. Poor Beatrice. Even at the tender age of eleven – which she must have been in 1910 – her mother was trying to get rid of her. To send her away, no doubt to distance the precious Trengrouse family name from the stigma that was attached to epilepsy back then. But at least Archie seemed to have cared about his daughter, who he fondly referred to as Beatie. At least she'd had one champion in an otherwise desolate existence. It was hard for me to understand Cordelia's hostile attitude to her daughter, as my own mother had always been so warm and caring. And seeing my sister with Gabby was love itself. But back then, the outward worry of stigma must have been greater than maternal love. For some people, at least.

I scanned the next few pages, in which Archie mainly seemed to be concerned with the repairs that Godwyne needed, as well as the finds he was choosing to put into what he called his 'special cabinet'. I put the diary back, put the box back on the shelf, and took down the one labelled '1916 – 1918'. By my reckoning, Beatrice would have been between seventeen and nineteen years old at this time.

A quick read-through told me that this diary centred on the First World War. While Archie didn't see any action, his nephews did, and they were both killed. His daughters were hardly mentioned in this journal, and neither was his wife. I put it back, and grabbed a file labelled '1920 – 1922'.

A quick skim-through of a page told me that I'd struck gold with this one.

> *March 1920. Why won't Cordy accept Beatie for being the wonderful child that she is? She has never warmed to her, and things are now at breaking point in the family. I was quite happy to give my consent to Beatrice and John for their wedding.*

Ah, I thought. *So Beatrice was twenty-one when she married.*

Now Cordy is sulking in London and is refusing to return. It really is all too much. I can't see why Beatie shouldn't have as happy a life as the rest of them...

So, I thought. *Cordelia was furious that Archie had given permission for Beatrice to get married. Perhaps she was planning on trying to keep her a spinster forever, so that she never had a chance to have children. But her husband put paid to that idea, so presumably she felt that she had to come up with another more underhand plan, especially when she found out that Beatrice was pregnant.*

I started reading again, but a noise at the door made me turn. Mrs Taylor was coming into the room.

Chapter Eighteen

'Ah, there you are, dear,' she said. *Dear?* I thought. Why was she being so much nicer to me than she was yesterday? But then, as I took in her weary face and the bags under her eyes, I realised the impact that poor Alexandra's death must have had on her. And I remembered the conversation I'd overheard between her and Mr Brentwood last night. If Mrs Taylor had suspicions that Alexandra hadn't just accidentally fallen, but had in fact been pushed, it must be agony for her to be unable to say anything. Especially as the manager of Godwyne had told her not to talk about it to anybody else.

'Hello, Mrs Taylor,' I said, putting the diary down. 'How are you?'

'I've been better,' Mrs Taylor said. 'It was a long night, last night. Poor, poor Lady Trengrouse. It's a tragedy what happened to her.'

I nodded, and wished so much that I could discuss things with her. Be more open, and say that I strongly doubted that Alexandra had fallen accidentally too. But I just couldn't. Mrs Taylor's loyalties clearly lay with the Trengrouse family, and I had no doubt that anything I confided in her would be passed straight on to them.

'Come and have some elevenses with us, Grace,' Mrs Taylor said. 'We must all stick together in tough times, and today is certainly one of those.'

I didn't feel I could refuse such an offer, so I stood up and picked up my bag.

As I exited the castle and made my way round to the staff dining room, I caught sight of an extremely expensive-looking red car on the driveway.

'Lord Edward's,' Mrs Taylor said, as she spotted me looking at it. 'Does love his cars, that one. Has a whole garage full of them. Not that I know much about vehicles, of course, but I believe one is called a California Spyder or something. Strange name. Priceless, apparently.'

'Wow,' I said. *Edward must be absolutely loaded if he's able to collect those kind of cars*, I thought. *Would this give him a motive for murder? Wanting to keep up the kind of flashy lifestyle he's used to? Oh dear, I'm going to suspect everyone here from now on, aren't I?*

Minutes later, I was sitting at the wooden trestle table in the staff dining room, flanked by Jesse and Zara. Mary was carrying a large teapot over, and Mrs Taylor walked over to fetch a jug of milk and jar of sugar. Hobnob was curled up in a basket in the corner. Mr Brentwood came in through the door, carrying a plate of nice-looking biscuits. Everyone's faces mirrored how I felt; shocked, grief stricken, and bewildered.

'Drink up, all,' Mary said, placing a mug in front of each of us. 'Have sugar in your tea today. You're going to need it.'

Quietly, we all got ourselves a drink.

'I just can't believe it,' Mrs Taylor kept saying, shaking her head. 'Poor Lady Trengrouse.'

'Yes, what an awful thing to happen,' Zara said.

'I'll never forget seeing her lying on the ground like that,' Jesse said.

When I looked at him, I saw that there were tears in his eyes.

'Listen,' Mr Brentwood said. 'This is a horrific turn of events. But the family is going to be the hardest hit, aren't they? They're going to need all of us to be strong, to carry on with our daily jobs, and to keep the castle running smoothly while they mourn the loss of Lady Trengrouse.'

There were murmurs and nodding heads at this.

Are they all going to be mourning her loss? I thought. I stared at Mrs Taylor, trying to work out what she was really thinking. *If one of them pushed her, that person certainly won't be mourning. This is a place of smoke and mirrors, secrets and lies. Who here can I actually trust?*

'Yes, an awful accident,' Mary said, dabbing her nose with a tissue. 'If you ask me, the family should have kept a much better watch on Lady Trengrouse. If she was given to wandering, then why didn't they take better care of her?'

For once, Mrs Taylor didn't reprimand Mary for speaking against the family. She just stared at her, wide-eyed, her expression unreadable.

'Are any of them back at the castle now?' I said.

Zara turned towards me.

'Yes,' she said. 'They all are. I was in the office when the car drove in early this morning, I saw it on the security camera.'

'And are the police here?' I said.

'Yes,' Zara said. 'They're talking to the family right now...'

A crash behind me made us all turn round. It was Will, banging the door open. He strode in and stood near to me. I could smell the alcoholic fumes on him immediately. His face was red and angry, and by his dishevelled state it looked as though he hadn't got any sleep at all. Hobnob immediately woke up and jumped onto the sideboard.

'You,' he said, his voice loud, pointing at me, 'are the one responsible for my grandmother's death. How fucking dare you come here, you snoopy little imposter. Everything was fine at Godwyne before you got here. And now you've ruined it all.'

Chapter Nineteen

'Hey,' Jesse said, standing up and taking a step towards Will. 'Now that's enough. I know you've had a bad shock, Will, but there's no point in taking it out on Grace. I think you need to go and cool off somewhere for a while.'

'You don't know, do you?' Will said, turning towards Jesse. 'You don't know the claims that sweet little Grace has been making since she arrived here at Godwyne, do you?'

Jesse sighed.

'What are you talking about?' he said.

'Grace here seems to think that she's a Trengrouse,' Will said, his voice a snarl. 'Mummy even had her dine with us last night. It seems that none of them can see through her façade. But I can.' He lowered his face towards mine until I could clearly see his bloodshot eyes and the spittle on his lips. 'And if you want my advice, Gracie, I would pack your bags now and get the hell out of here, before you get what's coming to you.'

'Right, that's it,' Jesse said, deftly catching hold of Will's arm and twisting it behind his back. 'Out you go, Mr Trengrouse. You should know by now, real men never speak to ladies like that.'

I watched, heart rate pounding, as Jesse marched the drunk man out of the dining room.

As I clenched my trembling fingers together, and tried to blink back the tears, I realised that four faces were all turned towards me, their eyes staring inquisitively.

'Are you all right, dear?' Mary said. 'It was very wrong of young Will to talk to you like that. I know he's in shock, but there's no excuse for that kind of behaviour.'

I tried to nod, but I couldn't move my head.

Zara put her arm round me.

'He's a brute,' she said. 'He always has been, at least ever since I came to work at Godwyne two years ago. I've been on the receiving end of several verbal attacks by Will, and it's always horrible. I've got more used to it now, learned how to tune him out.'

Mrs Taylor sighed.

'Yes,' she said, looking at me, her eyes kind. 'I'm always the first to defend the Trengrouses, after all, I've worked here for longer than the boys have been alive. But Will has always been the black sheep. And his behaviour has got worse over the years. And no matter what anyone does or says to him, he never changes. I don't know what's wrong with him; neither of his parents have ever acted like he does. I'm sorry he spoke to you like that, Grace.'

Mr Brentwood cleared his throat.

'Ah,' he said. 'Yes I agree, Will should know better at his age. I'm a little intrigued by his claims though, Grace. Is all that mumbling about you being related to the Trengrouses complete nonsense?'

I sat up a little, willing myself to start feeling normal again. Jesse returned to the room and resumed his place next to me on the bench.

'Took him back to his rooms to calm down,' he said. 'Sorry, Grace. He should never have spoke to you like that.'

I nodded. Everyone's kindness was making me feel better.

'Look,' I said, after a pause. 'The thing is, there's just an old myth in my family that's been handed down through the generations. It's not a big deal, and Will has taken it completely out of context.'

'Oh yes, and what's that then, dear?' Mary said, leaning forwards.

'Just that my sister and I are somehow distantly related to the Trengrouses,' I said, determined to underplay the situation as much as I could. The last thing I needed was any of the staff finding out about Alexandra's claims. My time at Godwyne was going to be hard enough, and although everyone around the table *appeared* to be nice, I no longer knew who were my enemies and friends at the castle.

'What do you mean, distantly?' Zara said.

'Oh, you know,' I wafted a hand in the air, 'fifth cousins ten times removed, or something. Nothing important.'

Was it my imagination, or was there a look of relief on Mr Brentwood's face?

'Ooh, a mysterious connection,' Mary said. 'How exciting.'

'No,' I gave her a small smile, 'not really. To be honest, Mary, I have other reasons for wanting the book I'm writing at Godwyne to be a success.'

I told them all about my niece Gabby, how she had cystic fibrosis, and how she was ill in hospital. When I started describing the expensive treatment that she needed in America, how it might save her life, and how my sister couldn't afford to send her, tears began to flow down my cheeks. It had been the most awful night, and it was turning out to be a very stressful day too.

I felt Jesse lean into me as I cried, and I found the warmth from his body strangely comforting. Zara still had her arm around me.

'And so you see,' I said between sniffs, 'I didn't come to Godwyne as some sort of Trengrouse imposter, as Will seems to think. I genuinely came because I want to write the best book I can. My agent says she will do everything she can to secure the best deal and advance for it, and that way I'm hoping to raise enough money to send Gabby to America.'

'You poor thing,' Mary said, reaching out to hold my hand. Mrs Taylor's eyes were sympathetic, and even Mr Brentwood's expression was less severe than usual. 'I'll make sure I buy the book when it comes out. Will that help, love?'

I nodded, and grinned through my tears.

'Yes,' I said. 'Thank you, Mary, that would be really lovely of you.'

After several biscuits and another cup of tea each, the break was over. I decided to stay behind after the others left, and help Mary clear the table and tidy up the room a bit. I was beginning to trust her the most out of everyone at the castle; there was something about her kindness that reminded me of my mother. It felt good to be near someone so stalwart and warm for a little while. Someone had obviously been reading a paper – a tabloid – and as I moved it from a bench to the sideboard I caught sight of some of the headlines. Something about the economy – which had apparently taken a slight downturn. A search for a missing fraudster who had been charged with swindling two businesses. A cheerful piece about a woman who'd bred the largest lop-eared rabbit in Britain. It was strange to think that life in the world went on while you were dealing with a calamity. That although Alexandra had died in such an awful way, people out there were just carrying on with their daily lives – completely unaffected.

I wasn't sure I'd be able to concentrate, but I had work to do, and I really needed to try and focus...

The next two days passed in a melancholy cloud. My fifth day at Godwyne started in a way that I was used to now; get up, get dressed, have a bit of breakfast, then make my way back to the library to trawl through more records. The police had come to speak to me the day before, and to protect my own skin, I'd decided not to show them Alexandra's note – a decision I was feeling very conflicted about.

I was on my way back towards the castle after eating a piece of toast and drinking a coffee. The sun was out for once, and I enjoyed its warm rays on my head and back. But the castle looked sinister now in my view, with all the serious-faced statues adorning the battlements, the Gothic spires rising up behind them, the cold grey stone. Even in the sun's rays, my opinion of it had changed since Alexandra's death. Everything about it now seemed ominous, unknown, and full of secrets. Walking across a patch of short grass, breathing in the delicious freshly cut smell, I waved to Jesse – who was on his lawnmower a few metres away – then kept close to the cold castle wall, and rounded a buttress on my way back to the main entrance. I was pretty confident in finding the Upper Library again with ease from there. The place was already becoming more familiar to me – I'd made my way up and down to it often now.

That's when I heard it, the almighty crack above me. I instinctively jumped to the side, as a giant statue hit the ground just where I'd been walking.

Chapter Twenty

'Oh my God, Grace, are you all right?' Jesse was running up behind me, as I wiped the shocked tears from my eyes. 'If you hadn't moved like you did, you'd be squashed right underneath that now. I looked up as soon as I heard the noise; I couldn't believe it when I saw it falling. It really did look like it was going to land on you.'

I couldn't move. I was shaking, just staring at the broken statue in front of me. Its impact on the ground had been hard enough to shake up the earth around it. Jesse was right, it was heavy enough to have ended my life. And my gut feeling told me that its sudden descent to earth had been intended for exactly that reason.

I felt Jesse's arm go round my shoulder; warm and comforting.

'I couldn't swear to this,' he went on, 'but I thought I saw someone up there on the battlements, going away, just after this giant thing fell. There was definitely some sort of movement up there. What the hell is going on here at Godwyne? Surely they couldn't have...' His words trailed off.

That bit of information made me move. I craned my head

back, and stared up at the row of spaced, squared openings. As far as I could see, no one was there. But then they wouldn't be now, would they? Whoever it was that was wreaking havoc at the castle was clearly trying not to get caught. Thought they could get away with causing destruction for their own ends. But I was aware of what they were doing, and so was Jesse now. But would we be able to stop them from doing anything else? From actually finishing me off?

'Fuck,' I said, my voice a whisper. 'It's happening already.'

'What?' Jesse said. 'What's happening?'

'Someone's trying to get me,' I said. And with that, I burst into tears again. The shock of the statue, on top of my niece being in hospital, Alexandra's death and Will's cruel words, was too much for me to cope with. I turned and sobbed into Jesse's shoulder, unable to stem my tears for what seemed like ages.

'Listen,' Jesse said eventually, when I was a bit calmer. 'Come with me. I'll make you a nice cup of tea, and you can tell me what the hell is going on. You're clearly in no state to work at the moment, and frankly I don't think you should be on your own right now.'

I let him lead me away from the castle, and off over the grass, through some trees and down a winding path towards a small, yellow-bricked cottage that I hadn't spotted since arriving at Godwyne. It was a pretty little thing, with ivy covering the walls and tall flowers waving in the breeze at the front.

'Welcome to my humble abode,' Jesse said, as we arrived at the red front door. 'When we get in, sit yourself down, and I'll put the kettle on.' He opened the door and then stepped back to let me enter first.

Minutes later, we were sitting opposite each other at his little wooden kitchen table. My sobs had stopped now, but I was feeling wretched and scared.

'So,' Jesse said, his eyes full of concern. 'What's going on?

You seem terrified, Grace, and I'm not surprised. Do you really think that someone pushed that statue off the battlements on purpose?'

I looked at him, my eyes swollen, trying to work out if I could trust this man. Usually, I'd go to Penny if I needed advice or a chat about something, but I obviously couldn't give her any more stress at the moment, what with Gabby being so ill in hospital. I desperately needed a sounding board, as my thoughts were freewheeling to the point that it felt like my head might explode, and at the moment it seemed like Jesse was my only option.

I took a deep breath, and then began to explain my situation, in fits and starts to begin with, then with the words flowing more fluently as I went on. I told him about what Alexandra had said to me after dinner on the first day I'd been at Godwyne, how she said she'd had proof that I was a direct descendant of Archie Trengrouse, and that I should come to her room later on to collect the birth and wedding certificates. I explained how I'd fallen asleep, only to be awoken by the awful scream, and had then seen poor Alexandra's dead body outside. I told him about finding a note from her that she'd hidden in my laptop, and how this proved to me that she'd been murdered, that in my view there was no way she'd accidentally fallen out of that window on a nightly wander, as the family seemed to want to say. And how as someone – or maybe more than one person – knew that I was apparently a direct descendant of Archie, they weren't afraid to end Alexandra's life to silence her, and were now apparently after mine. And all to apparently keep whatever money there was in the Trengrouse family.

Jesse was staring at me, his mouth slightly open.

'Well there's only one thing for it,' he said after a brief pause. He reached for his phone. 'We have to phone the police right now, Grace. If someone is trying to harm you, and if you suspect that Lady Trengrouse was murdered, then we have to let them know this instant.'

'No,' I said, my voice almost a shout. 'Please, Jesse, don't do that.'

'What?' He looked at me. 'Why not?'

'Because,' I said, 'I have no proof of any of this. Yet. But in my gut I know it's true. And I'm trying to stay low-key while I'm here, and away from the gazes of the Trengrouses. The only reason that I'm still here at the castle is my niece Gabby, and the fact that I desperately want to raise money to send her for the treatment she needs. If it wasn't for her, I'd have left first thing the morning after Alexandra was killed. If I can get some solid evidence that someone murdered her, then of course I'll go straight to the police. But until then, I have to pretend that I know nothing. Whilst trying to stay alive, obtaining evidence that I am actually descended from Archie, and researching material for my book. I'd also like to have a look for the jewels, as I'm now prepared to do anything to raise money to send my niece to America. Do you see?'

'Hmm,' Jesse said, a range of emotions struggling with each other on his face.

There was a pause.

'Fine,' he said. 'But I'm going to keep a close eye on you from now on, Grace, and help keep you safe. Okay? It broke my heart when I saw old Lady Trengrouse lying there on the gravel that night. She was my favourite out of the lot of them; she was always kind, always showed an interest in what I was doing. I can't believe she's gone. And the last thing I want is for anything to happen to you. I'd feel responsible, especially as I now know that you might be in danger. All right?'

'Thank you, Jesse,' I said, feeling my lips break into a smile. 'I would really appreciate that. So don't you think much of the other Trengrouses?'

'Not really,' Jesse said, a look of distaste on his face. 'Look, I'm a local boy, born and bred. And I've heard talk about them in the village. And what goes round about them is far from rosy.'

'Oh really?' I said, leaning forwards. Anything I could learn about the family's deep, dark secrets may well help me to figure out which one of them was after me. 'What are people saying about them?'

'Well I don't like to spread rumours,' Jesse said. 'And I could never say anything in front of old Margaret Taylor. But word has it that Edward Trengrouse is up to his ears in debt. Have you seen the amount of cars he's got? I don't know where he's getting the money for them, because as far as I know he's never done a day's work in his life. Lives off the castle estate, as far as I can see. Probably takes out loans to maintain his flashy lifestyle; that's my bet anyway. Always on the lookout for his next purchase, flashy bastard. And he's never been as nice as his mum was. Barely ever says hello if he sees any of us around the house or grounds.'

'That's interesting,' I said. 'I saw him in an expensive-looking red car a couple of days ago. So he'd certainly have a motive for not wanting to dilute whatever money there is, if he's dripping with debt.'

'Yep,' Jesse said. 'And that Will is apparently into gambling. I've got friends that have seen him in the bookies more times that they've had hot dinners. Not very good at it either, it seems. Maybe that's why he's always in such a mood. Drinks himself unconscious most nights too. I do the rubbish collection every week, and the amount of empty bottles he leaves in his bins is unreal.'

'God,' I said. 'So Will also has a strong reason not to want me around. Not that he's made any secret of that at all, but until now I couldn't understand what his motive was. To be honest, he seems to be the likely candidate for any harm done to me, as he hasn't exactly been subtle about his feelings since I arrived here. But would anyone be that blatant and obvious?'

'If you look up the word "blatant" in the dictionary, you'll find a picture of Will there,' Jesse said. 'I don't think he knows what subtle means. Doesn't mean that it's not him behind whatever's going on though, does it? Then you've got Howard of course,' he went on. 'Seems nice, but it's said in the village that he has at least one mistress on the go behind his wife's back. Probably more.'

'Really?' I said. Now this surprised me. 'Him and Mimi seem to make such a good couple.'

'Yep,' Jesse said. 'But generations of my family have worked at Godwyne for many years, and they've all said that the Trengrouse men have a reputation for womanising. Goes with the posh territory, doesn't it? They all used to be at it apparently, especially in the old days. Always having affairs with each other after dinner parties and balls, weren't they? Maybe Howard's inherited a taste for that kind of thing. And it must be an expensive job, trying to keep all his floozies happy.'

'Yes, maybe,' I said. Wow, so these must be some of the deep, dark secrets that Alexandra had hinted her family were harbouring. What else, I wondered, was there to find out about them? I was suddenly beginning to understand how much was going on behind the family's façade. They were as complex and corrupt as the best of them, and the problem was that they were used to having money to plough into whatever vices they had. No wonder it was annoying for them to have a random relative show up out of the blue who had the possibility of diluting whatever wealth was left...

'Helena's an airhead,' Jesse said. 'God knows where she keeps disappearing off to all the time. Hardly ever at the castle, not that Edward minds, he'd do anything for her. Doesn't mind lavishing gifts and money on her either, as far as I can see. The amount of shopping bags she comes back with are unreal. And then there's Sukie. Pardon my French, but she's just a bitch.'

I couldn't help smiling at that.

'Always complaining that I've missed a patch of grass, or that Mary's meals aren't hot enough, or that Margaret's missed a millimetre of dust in the living room, or that Zara hasn't added up some numbers correctly. Honestly, there's no pleasing that woman. And either she or her husband like a drink almost as much as Will does; the amount of bottles I collect from their apartments is incredible.'

I smiled. Then remembered the conversation I'd had with the family the night I'd arrived.

'Have you heard the rumour about old Archie burying some priceless family jewels in the garden?' I said, half expecting Jesse to laugh at this. 'Edward told me about it, and to be honest I was aware of the rumours before I arrived at Godwyne. He said that Archie buried loads of valuable things in the grounds because he got so sick of his wife and daughters' spending habits. That people have been looking for them ever since, but with no luck.'

'Yes, I know all about that,' Jesse said, no hint of mirth on his face. 'And if you ask me, I reckon it's true. I'm the groundsman here, right? So not much gets past me that goes on outside. And I've seen Will digging with my own eyes, several times. He usually waits till after dark – probably when he has a few drinks in him – then comes out with a shovel and starts making holes in my grass. Annoying bugger. I think some of the others have been at it too; Edward once had a whole patch dug up over by the orchard. Said it was for some archaeological reason, but if you ask me, he was looking for the jewels. And he dug round the old icehouse once, near the monastery ruins that Archie liked so much. Didn't find anything though, apart from a few worms. I've seen Helena out there with a spade a few times; didn't put much effort into it though, probably didn't want to break her nails. If Archie's family was anything like the Trengrouses who live in the castle now, then I don't blame him for burying the treasure, to be honest.'

'Wow, so people actually look for the jewels,' I said. 'That's interesting.'

'Yeah, they've been looking for years,' Jesse said. 'But no one's had any luck so far. I mean, Archie could have been playing a joke on the lot of them, pretended to have buried things, but I doubt it. There was a famous collection of valuables that past Trengrouses had collected or been given, like the French bracket clock that King Louis XIV gave to a past duke in the family, some eighteenth-century diamond earrings and rings, and lots of other bits. My dad told me that the collection has even been written about in the papers. But no one's seen any of these valuables since Archie died, and their disappearance caused quite a bit of a stir at the time. The newspapers have more details about it all.'

'I'll look them up again,' I said. 'Thanks, Jesse.'

We chatted on for a while, and then I caught sight of the time on the wall clock.

'Shit,' I said, jumping up. 'I better go and do some work. I've got so much to do. Thank you so much for looking after me, Jesse, I really appreciate it. I was in bits before, I don't know what I'd have done if you weren't there when that statue fell.'

'No worries,' Jesse said, also standing up. 'I'll walk you back up and make sure you get to the library safely, without anything else horrible happening. And I'll give you my number. Just call me if anything else strange happens, okay?'

I smiled and nodded, and minutes later we were walking back up the gravel path, me with Jesse's number on a scrap of paper in my pocket.

As we reached the entrance to the castle, Mrs Taylor came hurrying past, a box of cleaning products in her hands.

'Sorry, can't stop,' she said, walking quickly past us. 'I've just been told that I have to clean out Lady Trengrouse's room right now. Not sure if I understand why it has to be done so quickly, just days after she died, but who am I to question things?'

She walked off in front of us. Hobnob appeared from a doorway and started to follow her, but then thought better of it and sat down to watch Jesse and I.

'I've never heard her say anything even slightly critical about the family before,' Jesse whispered. 'She must be in a state. Bless old Margaret; she does work hard.'

I thought for a moment.

'I've got an idea,' I whispered back. Then I ran after Mrs Taylor.

'Ah, would you like some help cleaning out the room?' I said, catching up with her. 'I've got a few minutes before I need to start working again, and it sounds like you could do with some extra hands?'

Mrs Taylor stopped and looked at me.

'Would you mind, dear?' she said. 'Zara's only just told me that Lord Trengrouse wants this doing now, and I've already got so much more to do today, I don't know how I'm going to fit it all in...'

'Not at all,' I said. 'I'd be happy to help.' *And while I'm there*, I thought, *I can have a look for those certificates that Alexandra was telling me about. That's if whoever is after me hasn't taken them first...*

Chapter Twenty-One

I followed her to the west section of the castle; an area I'd not yet been in since arriving at Godwyne. Soon, now on the first floor, we turned down a corridor that was decorated in beautiful wallpaper; large white roses shone out at us from both sides. *So that's what Alexandra was talking about when she told me to follow the white roses,* I thought. *I don't think she was mad at all, no matter what the family say...*

'It's such a sad time,' Mrs Taylor said mournfully, as she opened a door at the end of the corridor. 'I never thought Lady Trengrouse's life would end like that.'

I shook my head as we entered the largest, most grand bedroom I'd ever been in in my life. A four-poster bed stood against one wall, long, thick golden curtains adorned the windows, and the furniture was so grand that it wouldn't have looked out of place in a royal palace. Gold and silver trinkets lay on the dressing table and shelves, and there was a bookcase packed with ancient-looking volumes.

'The whole thing really is horrific,' I said. 'And I can't see how she would be wandering around by herself that night, and manage to accidentally fall out of the window?' I was fishing for information, as I wanted to see whether Mrs Taylor would tell me anything more. I couldn't forget what I'd overheard her saying to Mr Brentwood the night before. But she just looked at me, and from the expression on her face, it looked like she was in agony.

'I find it hard to believe as well,' she said. But that was it. Her lips pursed firmly shut.

We got to work, packing Alexandra's belongings into the cardboard boxes that someone had already stacked neatly in one of the corners. *Strange that the family want her room obliterated quite so quickly*, I thought, picking up a pile of clothes from a large drawer. *Then again, not so strange, when you know everything that I do... Someone definitely wants to cover their tracks and get rid of any evidence to do with me. And if Edward was the one to give her that instruction, does that point to him being involved in some way? Although everyone in the family is a suspect now...*

We'd been working away for over half an hour, with me keeping an eye out for the certificates but with no luck, when I picked up a Bible that was lying in a drawer in a wooden cabinet on one side of the bed.

'Wow, this looks like an old book,' I said, opening it. Antique books had always fascinated me, I loved to visualise the many owners that they'd had.

'Probably an heirloom that's been handed down through the various Trengrouses,' Mrs Taylor said, stripping the sheet off the bed. 'They look after their wealth, that family.'

Indeed they do, I thought. I flicked through the thin pages, coming at last to the inside of the back cover. I blinked. There seemed to be some sort of subtle division along it, that was barely perceptible to the naked eye. The idea hit me. I turned around, so that Mrs Taylor couldn't see what I was doing, then slid my fingers into the gap. They nudged against paper. Very slowly and carefully, I withdrew two, folded, yellowing sheets, and opened one quickly to take a look.

Marriage solemnised at... I read. Beatrice Trengrouse...

I quickly folded it up, then pocketed the two bits of paper. I turned round, fearful that Mrs Taylor would have been watching what I was doing. But she was busy pressing the sheet down into a box and couldn't have seen much from where she was standing. I was utterly thrilled to have found the certificates. I couldn't believe my luck; I'd been sure that whoever hated my presence at the castle would have got there first and destroyed them. But then maybe they weren't aware of the fact that many people throughout history had hidden documents in old books such as the Bible. Perhaps they'd gone through Alexandra's room after her death, and hadn't been able to find them?

I stayed to help Mrs Taylor pack up for a while, not wanting to leave her with such a big job to do by herself when she had so many other things to be getting on with, or to make such an obvious exit after finding the certificates. Eventually, when there wasn't much more to do and most of the boxes were neatly packed, I made my way to the Upper Library. I had a lot of work to do, I thought. And my main job was to look up the dates written on the certificates in Archie's diaries, and see what he had to say about his daughter's wedding and his grandson's baptism. And also to trace the lost collection of valuables that Jesse had told me about...

Chapter Twenty-Two

Up in the library, I spread out the wedding and birth certificates on my desk – after making sure that the camera on the ceiling above would not be able to record my movements. Both bits of paper were in bad condition, and the birth certificate was torn down one fold. But there was no mistaking the evidence that they held. Beatrice's marriage had taken place in 1920 and Jacob's baptism took place in 1921 when he was one month old. He'd been as legitimate as Ottilie's son, and therefore – as the older boy by the eldest daughter – should have been the heir to Godwyne Castle, by the standards of his time. However, this had not happened, due to Cordelia's interference. All I needed to do now, was to somehow trace my own birth back to Jacob, and I would have solid evidence of my direct family link to Archie and the castle.

My phone pinged, and I picked it up. It was a message from Penny. My heart started thumping. *Oh please, not more bad news about my niece...*

Hi Grace, I read. Just wanted to let you know the good news – Gabby's condition has stabilised, and I'm allowed to be with her for quite a few hours today. Sorry for the rushed message, will send more later xxx

Phew, I thought, feeling a great stress begin to leave my body. This was excellent news. And it also meant that me drumming up the funds for the trip to America – while still crucial – wasn't quite as burningly urgent as I'd thought it was after talking to my sister just after my niece was taken into hospital. An extra few days of investigating was exactly what I needed...

Chapter Twenty-Three

It was my ninth day at Godwyne, and I was raking through reports of the Trengrouses' collection of valuables. I'd found out a lot in the previous few days, but there were still holes that I needed to fill in. I wanted to put the pieces of everything together, in the manner of a mental jigsaw, until I understood what exactly had gone missing and when, and then the second part of the jigsaw would be to search through Archie's records to see if I could find any clues as to what he did with it. Completing this puzzle, together with the one about my own birthright, would help me to work out what course of action to take next.

The third jigsaw I had to put together, the sinister and awful one, was to find out who was responsible for Alexandra's death. Presumably the same person who'd pushed that statue off the battlements a few days earlier; if Jesse was correct, and there had been someone up there. Of course, it could have just been an accident. A coincidence that I was standing under it when it fell; after all, the castle was very old, and bits of it were bound to be decaying. But gut instinct told me that it hadn't been an accident.

And while I was terrified of being hurt – or even killed – while I was at Godwyne, I was now also filled with a sustained, red-hot anger at the injustice of Alexandra's death, and I knew that this was driving me to do the best that I could to unearth her killer, and also to somehow raise the money that Penny and Gabby needed. It was like I had tunnel vision now; I had never cared about anything so much before in my life. This feeling had grown with every day that passed. The Trengrouses were a family who seemed at odds with each other; whereas to me, family was everything. Especially since my mum and dad had passed away. I was prepared to do anything to help Gabby, and also to bring justice for Alexandra, who I now realised was also a close relative of mine. No one else seemed to be interested in investigating her death as anything else but an accident, so I would bloody well do it for her on my own.

The police had been fairly uninterested, in my opinion. I still hadn't heard the results of their investigation, but their presence at Godwyne had waned to nil over the last few days, and I found it hard to believe that they thought it was anything more than an accident if they weren't conducting more vigorous enquiries.

An hour and a half later, after much laptop research, I'd found out some very interesting information that I hadn't seen before. Luckily, as a member of the British Library, I had easy, remote access to archives – and I'd always found this a crucial help to my research. Never more so than now...

Family Search for Lost Treasure was the headline that the *Daily Mercury* chose to run with.

Lady Cordelia Trengrouse says she has no idea where the family's historic collection of jewels and other priceless artefacts could be. 'My husband Archibald always loved archaeology,' Lady Trengrouse said. 'And as a parting gift – almost as a game for us – he decided to bury part of the children's inheritance somewhere in the grounds of the castle. He did a very good job of hiding it, as none of us have found the collection yet.'

An article published a year later by the same newspaper, said:

Armed Guards Called in as Treasure Hunters Flock to Godwyne Estate... Since news about the buried jewels in Godwyne Castle's estate became public last year, the Trengrouse family have reported much trouble with criminally-minded treasure seekers coming onto their property to look for the priceless artefacts. Much of their grounds have been ruined by the selfish hunters, who have dug up many flowerbeds in their searches for the treasure that was allegedly buried by Lord Archibald Trengrouse. But no one has located it as yet...

I couldn't find any more newspaper coverage after the second article, other than the pieces I'd already read before arriving at Godwyne. Clearly, the stampede to the castle that Cordelia had initiated by going public with news about the buried treasure had made her media shy after that. And without the public interest, knowledge about Archie's buried stash had faded away, other than in the minds of the Trengrouses, and those who worked for them on the estate.

Noticing my rumbling stomach, I glanced at my phone and realised that I'd completely missed lunch. It was 3.46pm. I decided that the best course of action would be to take my belongings back to my room, and then go in search of Mary, and see if she had any leftovers anywhere that I could eat.

Making my way – now with ease – back to my bedroom, I opened the door and was about to place my laptop on the bed, when a folded piece of white paper caught my eye. It was so neatly placed in the middle of the duvet, that in an instant I knew someone else had been in my room and put it there. I knew for a fact that there hadn't been anything at all on the bed when I'd left the room, as I could remember that pulling the duvet into position was the last thing I'd done before setting off to the library.

My heart now pounding, I picked up the paper. I had a bad feeling; Alexandra was dead, and I couldn't think of anyone else who'd need to send me a private message. Plus it was beyond worrying that someone had been in my room again behind my back…

I unfolded the paper, and stared at the capital letters inside:

GO HOME OR DIE.

Chapter Twenty-Four

Jesse, I thought. *I need to go and find him right now.* He was the only other person at Godwyne who knew what was going on, and he'd said that he wanted to protect me. That he now felt strangely responsible for my safety.

Stuffing my laptop into my travel bag – there was no way I was ever leaving that in my room without me from now on – I grabbed my handbag, stuffed the horrible note into it, and headed out of the door. He'd given me his number a few days ago, and we'd been getting closer every day – stealing chats here and there – but there was no point in just texting him, as I wanted to actually be *with* him; have another sane human being who understood what I was going through by my side. Feel the comfort of human closeness, not just tap away at a device. Soon, I was running down the nearest set of stone stairs. Jesse would most probably still be outside, I thought. That seemed to be where he spent most of his time, other than when he grabbed a quick meal. He couldn't be far, and if he was, I'd just ring him and ask him to hurry back to the castle...

Arriving on the ground floor – and for once not stopping to

stroke Hobnob – I quickly made my way towards a side door, opened it, and walked straight into Howard.

'Hi, Grace,' he said. I could see that his father, Edward, was just behind him. 'Are you rushing off somewhere?'

'Oh,' I said. 'I just need to, er, do something.' Although my heart was pounding, and I had no idea if one of the two men standing in front of me was Alexandra's killer, I remembered my manners.

'I'm so sorry about what happened to Lady Trengrouse,' I said. I hadn't seen much of them since that day – thank God. Even though she'd told me to call her Alexandra, I knew that I couldn't very well refer to her as that when I was talking to other family members. It would sound too disrespectful.

'Yes,' Howard said with a sigh. 'None of us can believe it, can we, Daddy?' He turned to Edward, who stepped forward. 'We're still in shock.'

'No.' Edward shook his head. 'I can't even count the amount of times I've had to go and find Mother over the last few years, after she'd gone wandering off somewhere. If only we'd kept a better eye on her, especially that night. I knew that her mind had begun to go, but I hadn't realised to what extent.'

Now this sounded like a disingenuous thing for him to say, I thought. Because – in my view – there hadn't seemed much wrong with Alexandra's mind at all. Yes, she was old. But that didn't mean she was bonkers, did it? Why, I wondered, are they both so unquestioning about her death? It was weird. Surely the whole family can't be in cahoots together?

'Yes,' I said. 'I've heard people say that she'd started to wander. Although I must say that when I talked to her, I thought she was lovely.'

'Mmm,' Edward said. 'Mother always had a good way with people. Always knew how to put them at ease. It was sad to see her going downhill over the last few years; her mind was so vibrant once.'

'Yes I can see that,' I said. 'But...'

A loud scream cut across my words.

'Stop it, Will.' It was Mimi's voice. 'You've been drinking again, haven't you? God you're foul when you get like this.'

'Let me get past.' Will's voice was a roar. 'Let me go and find that money-grabbing little shit of a woman.'

The three of us looked round to see Will and Mimi coming over the grass. Mimi was trying to grab hold of his arm, but Will – his face purple – was pushing her away each time. When he saw me standing there, he charged towards the door.

'Oh dear,' Howard murmured. 'You better go inside, Grace. I'll handle this.'

'Why?' I said, alarm rising swiftly inside me. 'What's going on?'

'Granny's last will was read to us half an hour ago,' Howard said. 'After we heard that her death has been ruled an accident. It seems she had it changed on the afternoon of your arrival. She's left you something, although so far we haven't found out exactly what. I'm afraid my brother is rather furious about the whole thing. It's why Daddy and I were just on our way to see you. We wanted to talk to you about it, explain that Will's got a bit of a bee in his bonnet...'

'What?' I said. 'Surely she can't have done that?'

'You,' Will said to me, spitting out the word, 'are a leech and a parasite. How dare you just turn up at Godwyne and wheedle your way into Granny's trust like that? You don't deserve any of her money. You don't deserve anything from us. You're not a Trengrouse, and I've had enough of this half-baked idea that you're somehow related to us. Just fuck off back to London, will you? And stop telling people that you're related to my family.'

His words were slurred, his eyes as bloodshot as the last time

I'd seen them. After the last nine days, with all the stress and trauma that had gone with them, his animosity stoked up the fiery anger in me that had been burning since I'd seen Alexandra's dead body. I'd had enough of the way he'd treated me since I'd arrived at the castle, enough of his rudeness and hostility. And now that I'd seen the certificates Alexandra had been looking after, something inside me had changed. I was no longer prepared to put up with his menacing attitude.

'I'm afraid I can't do that, Will,' I said, my tone icy.

'What the fuck are you talking about?' he said, lunging towards me. Howard stepped in front of him, while Edward – I noticed – stayed still, just watching his son.

'I mean, I can't stop telling people that I'm part of your family,' I said, unable to stop the words coming out. The ones I hadn't planned to say to any of the family for a good, long while. 'I now have proof that I am related to you, actually. And more than that, it turns out that I'm rather more closely related to you than I suspected, Will. Which I'm sure you'll be overjoyed about. I'm a direct descendant of Archie Trengrouse too.'

Chapter Twenty-Five

Will stopped talking, and Howard, Edward and Mimi all turned towards me, shock on their faces.

'What on earth are you talking about, Grace?' Edward said eventually. 'I mean, it's been a hard day for all of us. But *really*.' His eyes were hard.

'I'm directly descended from Beatrice, Archie's daughter,' I said. 'Her son Jacob was my great grandad. And although there's been an almighty cover-up of this information, I've still found it out. I'm very sorry if any of you are disappointed by this revelation, but it's true, so there we are.' I purposefully didn't mention that Alexandra had told me about it, or anything about her having the certificates, as her killer could be any one of them, and I was becoming aware that I'd probably played too much of my hand already.

There was a pause, while the four of them tried to make sense of my words.

At that moment, I saw Jesse – carrying a large spade on his back – walking across the grass about two hundred metres away.

'I'm so sorry,' I said to them. 'Do excuse me, but there's something I need to do.' I couldn't take in the revelation about

Alexandra's will. That would have to wait for later. Sorting out what to do about the awful note left in my room took priority.

Seconds later, I'd caught up with Jesse.

'Grace,' he said. He caught sight of my face. 'Shit, what's happened now? Are you all right?' He looked over at the castle.

'No, not really,' I said. I was aware that the four of them – Edward, Mimi, Howard and Will – would be watching our every move. Wondering about my strange behaviour – unless it was one of them who wrote the note... *Oh look,* I thought, a movement catching my eye. *There's Helena too, walking over the grass to join the merry throng... The whole lot of them give me the creeps.* 'Ah, is there somewhere private that we could go to talk? I've got something to show you.'

'Yep, no problem,' Jesse said. 'Come with me.'

Ten minutes later, we were both in his mud-splattered Land Rover, turning out of the estate's long drive, and right onto a country lane.

'Where are we going?' I said.

'To a nice little pub I know,' Jesse said, looking over at me. 'You look as though you could do with a drink, Grace. And it will do you good to get out of that place for a while. I always start feeling like I'm going mad if I stay there for too long with no break. And if you've got some important things to say, then the further we are away from Godwyne the better. Walls have ears in that place.'

'Good,' I said, feeling weak. 'Yes, I could do with a drink or two, if I'm honest. My head's spinning, Jesse. So much has happened, and it's hard to take it all in.'

For the tenth time since getting into the car, I bent down and checked that I had my travel bag – containing my precious laptop – and handbag with me. Since there weren't any locks on the doors in the castle, I had no doubt that someone would go snooping round my room again whilst I was out. And the only things they would find were changes of clothes and a phone charger, as I had all my valuables with me. It was horrible to think that someone there was so sneaky and underhand; there was a real sense of invasion when someone let themselves into your private space. But whoever it was, they would be sorely disappointed, I thought.

Seeing the trees, beautiful meadows and old stone walls rush by was like a balm for my painful thoughts. Such a sense of freedom, after being bound up in the dark goings-on at Godwyne. Proof that life existed beyond its walls. That there was more out there than the control of the upstairs, downstairs existence that went on in Godwyne, and the strange and sinister atmosphere of secrecy and subterfuge. Nature was the opposite to that; free, beautiful and accessible to all. Never any smoke and mirrors with plants, trees, flowers and fields.

We didn't talk much during the drive, but for some reason I felt comfortable with Jesse; it was as though we'd known each other much longer than just nine days.

About twenty minutes later, the car slowed down and we turned off the road and into a little village; a sign told me it was Bostow. I could see the sea from where we parked, next to an ancient-looking pub called The White Anchor. Its old bricks had been restored in many places, and the front door was much lower than the ones installed in modern buildings. Just the sort of place I liked. In a little while, we were ensconced in a booth, pints of lager in front of us, with Jesse looking at me with concern in his eyes.

'Grace,' he said. 'What's happened? You look terrified.'

'Well,' I said. 'Look at this.'

I retrieved the note from my handbag, and spread it out on the table for him to see.

'Christ,' Jesse said, shaking his head slowly. 'This is going from bad to worse. You're not safe in that castle. You need to get out of there. Please, think about letting me phone the police?'

'I can't do that,' I said. 'Not yet. I've already let the family know more about what I've discovered than I'd planned to.'

I told him about the incident just before, the shock about Alexandra leaving me something in her will, and Will's vile reaction to it. How I'd got angry when he'd told me that I was a leech and a parasite, and had admitted that actually, I was a direct descendant from Archie. Went over how I'd found Beatrice's wedding certificate, and her son Jacob's birth certificate in Alexandra's room when I was helping Mrs Taylor to pack up her things; a fact I'd already divulged to him during our previous chats.

'Wow,' Jesse said. 'So they know now. How did they take it? You saying all that?'

'They were speechless,' I said. 'They probably think I'm mad, and am making it up, unless any of them were already privy to what Alexandra knew.'

'Okay,' Jesse said. 'So let me get this straight. You already found the certificates, which is basically the start of completely proving how you're related to the Trengrouses. Then you find this bloody horrible note, and are told that Lady Trengrouse left you something in her will. This is all insane, Grace.'

'I know,' I said. 'I feel like I'm in a dream, Jesse. Actually, more of a nightmare. My sister says that my niece Gabby has stabilised, which is great news. But she still needs to go to America for treatment. I feel that I'm so close to somehow raising the money that they need. If I can just hang on a bit longer at Godwyne, maybe wait and hear what it is that Alexandra left me in her will, then I'll have what I need and I can get out of there. I don't care if the hook of the book puts a bad light on the Trengrouses now, I'm planning to write about the cover-up of Beatrice. It will make compelling reading and

I'll get a good deal. The thing is, if we go to the police, then it will change everything. The family would hate me even more. I'm sure that the police wouldn't be able to do much about one nasty note anyway, and I wouldn't be able to finish my research. I think it's better if I bide my time a bit longer, and see what else I can find out.'

'I don't know,' Jesse said, shaking his head. He was looking worried. 'I don't think someone is playing games with you here, Grace. I think they're serious. Look what happened to Lady Trengrouse?'

'I know,' I said with a sigh. 'I'm in danger, for sure. But I hate the thought that whoever the evil person – or people – behind all this is, they could scare me off by making me fearful enough, before I've uncovered the truth about everything. I want to do it for Alexandra's sake, as well as for Gabby's. Alexandra lost her life trying to tell me who I really am. And I don't want her to have died for nothing.'

Jesse nodded.

'Yep,' he said. 'I can understand that. But I don't think it's safe for you to sleep in the castle anymore, Grace. I'd already come to that conclusion anyway, but this information makes me certain. I was going to suggest this idea to you at some point today, but now I feel that you have no choice.'

'What idea?' I said.

'I've got a spare room at my cottage,' Jesse said. 'And I think you should move into it for the remainder of your stay at Godwyne. We can lock and bolt the front door every night – and even if I'm out doing my guard duty you can still lock the place up – and you'll be much safer there, than in the middle of the spider's web with all the others. What do you think?'

A huge sense of relief washed through me.

'Oh, Jesse, I would really like to do that, if it's okay with you?' I said. 'I could keep working in the library during the day;

I think I'll be safe there as there's a security camera in there which would capture anyone doing anything horrible.'

'Hmm,' Jesse said. 'That's a point. The castle is riddled with cameras since Edward had them all fitted last year after the break-in. Do you think one of them might have picked up whoever left that note in your room?'

'That's a thought,' I said, leaning forward. 'And there's more, Jesse. They might also show Alexandra with someone the night she died. The police have probably already looked into it, but I would like to see for myself. How would I find out?'

'Well, the screens that show everything that's going on in the castle are in the office, where Mr Brentwood and Zara work,' Jesse said. 'You could ask one of them to have a look?'

I nodded.

'But what should I tell them?' I said. 'I don't really want anyone else to know about the note yet.'

'Just make up some sort of excuse,' Jesse said. 'Say that you think you dropped something important in a corridor, but you can't find it, and you want to see the footage in case it shows you leaving it somewhere. Or say you sometimes sleepwalk, and you want to see the footage to find out if you've been doing it at Godwyne. Just think of something, Grace.'

'Okay,' I said, immediately racking my brains, wondering what excuse I could come up with that would be even vaguely believable. 'Good idea.'

We chatted on for a while, firstly mulling over who could be behind the notes and if they were potentially responsible for Alexandra's demise too. Each member of the family – we decided – were potential suspects at this stage. All of them held secrets – as often discussed by Jesse and his fellow villagers – and every one of them had cause to want more money than the wealth they already seemed to possess. Then Jesse told me a bit about the area, how he'd grown up in Bostow, which was the nearest village to the castle. His mum worked in a school and his dad was also a gardener. He said he'd been engaged to a local girl for a year, but she'd called it off nine months ago, and since then he'd chosen to throw himself into his work and forget about relationships altogether.

I was really enjoying the brief reprieve from the castle, the slice of normality that a relaxed pub setting could bring. I was drinking in the familiar smell of stale beer that was ubiquitous to any drinking establishment in the UK, and the delicious waft of chips coming from nearby tables. It was all so normal, and so comforting. And Jesse seemed to be such a straightforward and honest person; being with him was an antidote to the secrets, lies and subterfuge that was going on at Godwyne. I'd found that every day I was warming to him more, looking forward to seeing him. And I felt repelled by the idea of returning to the castle, but I knew that I must. For my sister and niece's sake...

My phone – lying on the table in front of me – pinged into life. I could tell from the number – having had frequent contact with Mr Brentwood in the run-up to my arrival at the castle – that it was someone from Godwyne calling me.

'Hello?' I said, suddenly feeling nervous. Surely nothing else could have happened since Jesse and I had left?

'Ah, Miss Haythorpe,' Mr Brentwood said. 'I do hope I'm not disturbing you, but I have a Mr Murphy here, who wants to speak to you. He was Lady Trengrouse's solicitor. He says that there is a matter of utmost importance that he must discuss with you today.'

I assured Mr Brentwood that I would be back at the castle soon, and would come and find Mr Murphy as soon as I arrived. As I rang off and looked up at Jesse, only one thing came to mind that would be of interest to the solicitor: Alexandra's will. And whatever it was that she'd left me...

Chapter Twenty-Six

'Ah, Miss Haythorpe.' Mr Brentwood did a small canter towards me. 'There you are.' He was, I noticed, looking slightly more ruffled than normal. And was it my imagination, or were his eyes cold when they looked at me? What was all that about? 'Mr Murphy is waiting for you in the study that adjoins my office.'

'Thank you, Mr Brentwood,' I said, giving him a small smile. 'I'll go straight there now.' I looked at Jesse, who was walking up behind me, jangling his car keys in his hand. He gave me an encouraging nod.

As I walked through the main castle entrance, and turned left in the direction of the office, an unmistakable figure rose up out of a leather armchair. It was Sukie. And if looks could kill, I'd have fallen down dead at that moment.

'I'd like to come in to see the solicitor with you, Grace?' she said, turning and moving off towards the door to Mr Brentwood's headquarters. 'I'm sure my mother-in-law wouldn't have minded. Might have expected you to be accompanied by a member of the family, in fact.'

'Oh,' I said, taken aback. 'Ah, I'm not really sure...'

I followed her through the incredibly tidy office, with its huge screen that showed multiple shots of the castle and grounds. Zara was working at a side desk. She looked up and smiled when she saw me.

Mr Murphy, when he appeared at the door of the study, put an end to Sukie's request.

'Oh no, Lady Trengrouse,' he said. 'I'm terribly sorry, but this is a matter that I must speak to Grace about in private.'

Sukie's eyes widened, but her well-trained face remained passive.

'Very well,' she said, before turning, glaring at me, then sweeping out of the office again.

Mr Murphy, a short, round man, gestured towards a chair.

'Please, do sit down, Miss Haythorpe,' he said, as he lowered himself into the chair behind the old desk. He reached up, took his spectacles from his head, and placed them on his nose. 'Right, now where are we...' He shuffled through some papers, retrieved an envelope from near the top of the pile, and withdrew some documents from it.

'As you may have heard by now,' he said, peering at me over his glasses, 'Lady Alexandra Trengrouse called me over, just hours before her death in fact, and asked me to amend her will. She said that she had a very special reason for doing that, and that reason was you.'

I could feel my mouth hang open slightly at that.

'I worked with Lady Trengrouse for many years,' Mr Murphy went on. 'And I came to consider her a personal friend, not just a client. She was a wonderful lady, even if she wasn't always treated as such by some people. I should perhaps point out, at this stage, that I don't work for any other member of the Trengrouse family.'

I nodded. I was beginning to trust Mr Murphy. If he saw

Alexandra for who she really was, not just some batty old lady, then I liked him already.

'From what I understand, Lady Trengrouse – Alexandra that is – had already found out that you were related to her before you arrived at Godwyne Castle,' Mr Murphy went on. 'And she was very excited, but also fearful, about meeting you. She always said that no one could be trusted in this place, and now – given what's happened – I fear she may have been right.'

He looked down for a moment. *His grief at her passing seems genuine,* I thought. *Strange how only the staff and people who worked for her seem affected. The family, not so much...*

'She'd already asked me to come over, we had a prior arrangement, you see,' he said. 'And once she'd seen you – at lunchtime apparently, on the day that she died – she said she was sure that she wanted to go ahead and change her will. She was determined to leave you something in it, you see. For many years, Lady Alexandra struggled with the attitudes of her immediate family. I can't disclose too much, of course, but suffice to say, she always felt that Beatrice and Jacob's descendants deserved to at least be included in the Trengrouse fortune, along with Edward, Susannah and all the rest of them. This was something she felt very strongly about. She felt you deserved it more than the rest.'

I nodded. Wow, this was amazing news to hear.

'Right.' Mr Murphy looked down at the top document in his hands. 'Let's see. Lady Alexandra has bequeathed five hundred thousand pounds to you.'

I gasped so sharply that it hurt my throat. Mr Murphy looked up and smiled.

'I can imagine that this is quite a shock to hear,' he said. 'Hopefully in a good way.'

I smiled as I felt tears sting my eyes. Oh, the wonderful lady. She couldn't have known anything about my niece Gabby, and how ill she was, and how she needed to get to America for the treatment. But by leaving me this money, she was effectively saving Gabby's life. I wanted to jump up and hug Mr Murphy for being the bearer of this wonderful news. I couldn't believe it. And I couldn't wait to ring Penny. After all, my sister was also a direct descendant of Archie's – although she didn't know it yet – and was entitled to the inheritance as much as me. But I was happy to give it all to her, if it meant that Gabby had a chance of living a normal life.

'Lady Alexandra also wrote a letter that she wanted me to give you...' Mr Murphy stopped and sighed. 'On the event of her death. I can't help feeling that she suspected her end was near...'

I nodded.

'I feel that too,' I said. 'It's as though she was almost planning for what happened. Putting steps in place from beyond the grave.'

'Yes,' he said quietly. 'She really was a remarkable woman.' His expression became angry. 'And I hope that the police open another inquiry into her death. The accidental verdict is quite shocking. Sorry,' he said, looking up at me. 'I shouldn't have said that.'

I shook my head.

'It's fine,' I said. 'I feel the same way.'

He gave me a small smile.

'Here,' he said, pushing the unopened envelope across the desk. 'This is for you.'

I picked it up, tore it open, unfolded the thick paper, and began to read the words. Not out loud though, as I wasn't sure what she had to say.

My dear Grace, Alexandra had written. I do hope this letter finds you well. If you are reading it, then I fear I have already made my exit from the world. Please don't be alarmed at what I have to say, but you need to know all this for your own protection. Firstly, enjoy your inheritance. Put it to good use. I know you will. Secondly, be very careful at Godwyne. Things are not all as they seem; not with the family, or the staff. I know you will dig deeper into your research, until you understand what I mean. I only got so far, but I could never find out the crucial link because my eyesight failed me. There is evil afoot in the castle, Grace, and you must be the one to put a stop to it once and for all. Dramatic as this may sound, it's incredibly important. Restore the Trengrouse seat to its former glory, and get rid of the rotten aspects that are pulling it down and ruining it. You know who you are now, and this is your right. Don't give up halfway through, stay the course, and resolve everything with finality. But always be on your guard; especially now, as word about my bequeathing you a gift will get out. And find the damn jewels that Archie hid. It's about time someone did. Do this for me, Grace. For Beatrice, Jacob and the rest of those who've been ousted. And more importantly, do it for yourself. I'll be looking down, helping you on your journey, never fear about that. Love forever and good luck, Alexandra.

As I looked up at Mr Murphy, tears were rolling down my cheeks.

'Thank you for giving this to me,' I said, my voice a whisper.

'No problem at all,' he said. 'Now, there's just one more thing, Miss Haythorpe. As per usual, it will take at least eight or nine months to execute the will...'

'What?' I said, sitting up. 'No, it can't take that long.' Images of Gabby in her hospital bed flashed through my mind.

'I'm sorry, Miss Haythorpe,' Mr Murphy said, frowning slightly. 'It is always a complex process, settling an estate. I thought you were pleased with Lady Alexandra's gift?'

'Oh,' I said. 'I am.' I told him all about my niece, and how she desperately needed to get over to America, and how – when he'd told me about it – the money had seemed like a lifesaver for her.

'I see,' he said, nodding. 'I'm so sorry, there's not much I can do to hurry the process up. But I will do my best.'

I nodded, thanked him, and he told me he would be in touch.

As I said goodbye and left the study, feeling more dazed than I ever had, I walked straight into Sukie, who had no doubt been standing very close to the door.

'Grace,' she said, as though my name was a dirty word. 'How did it go? What did Mr Murphy say to you?'

'Oh, you know,' I said, determined to keep things vague. There was no way that I was going to let Sukie know what the solicitor had told me. 'Alexandra's kindly left me something in her will.'

'Yes,' she said. 'And what exactly is that?'

'I'm so sorry, Sukie,' I said, sidling past her, 'I'm in a bit of a rush, I have so many things to do. Do you mind if we chat later?'

No doubt Sukie's finishing school training stopped her from telling me exactly what she thought of me at that moment, but the look she gave me had daggers in it.

'Of course, Grace,' she said, through gritted teeth. 'I will make a point of coming to find you later, so that we can continue this conversation.' She strode past me, through the office, and out into the big entrance hall.

I breathed out. Being near that woman always made my whole body tense, I realised. I didn't trust her one bit.

Now, I just had one more thing to do here.

'Mr Brentwood,' I said, passing Zara at her desk and going straight to him. 'I have a small favour to ask of you. On the night of Alexandra's death, I think I dropped a very precious necklace somewhere in the corridors, either on my way down to see what was happening, or on my way back up. I've searched for it everywhere, but I just can't find it. And to me, it really is priceless, I couldn't do without it. I was wondering if you might let me have a look at the CCTV from that night, just so I can see if I can spot myself dropping it somewhere?' It was a white lie, and a long shot, but it was worth giving it a go if I could just take a look at the footage...

Mr Brentwood's brow creased.

'Oh,' he said, giving a sigh. He looked up at my face and must have seen desperation there. 'Very well,' he said. 'The memory stick with that day's data on it would be in this drawer over here.' He got up and walked over to a small filing cabinet. 'Do you have a laptop that you could plug the stick into?' He pulled the drawer open.

I nodded. 'Yes I do,' I said, watching him stare at a box in the drawer that was divided into several sections. After a pause, he began lifting up other memory sticks and staring at the dates on them.

'That's strange,' he said, turning to Zara. 'That particular memory stick isn't here. Has anyone borrowed it?'

Zara looked up, and shook her head.

'No, not that I know of,' she said. 'The police asked for it, and I'm pretty sure they returned it the following day. Other than that I have no idea.'

Mr Brentwood turned back to the drawer and inspected each and every memory stick in there. Then he turned towards me.

'I'm very sorry, Grace,' he said. 'But the CCTV recordings from the night that Lady Alexandra died seem to have gone missing.'

Chapter Twenty-Seven

Shit, I was thinking, as I wound my way through the castle to the Upper Library, handbag and laptop in tow. *That's a bit of a coincidence, isn't it? That the CCTV evidence that might show Alexandra's killer has gone missing?* Although if the police have already looked at it then maybe there's nothing of interest on there. Or perhaps there is, something small, and they missed it. But either way, the fact that it was gone seemed like a deliberate act of sabotage, an attempt – by Alexandra's murderer – to cover their tracks, to stop anyone from finding out who they were. Perhaps in case someone else looked at it and saw something that had been overlooked. But who could it be behind this?

Will would be my first choice, purely because he'd been so vile to me since my arrival at Godwyne, I thought, entering the library. But then, it all seemed a bit too obvious if it was him. Surely you wouldn't publicly act like that *and* be the killer? Unless you were adopting the age-old trick of hiding in plain sight... Was it another member of the family? Sukie? She hated me enough, her glare said it all. She clearly thought that I was as much of an imposter as her son believed me to be. Or was it another Trengrouse?

I couldn't forget what Alexandra had written to me in her letter; that things weren't as they seemed, with the family *or* the staff. Now that was a horrible thought, because it meant I had to suspect Mr Brentwood, Mrs Taylor, Mary, Zara and even Jesse, as well as the Trengrouses. But what on earth would their motives be? Did Mr Murphy fall into that category too? Where should my suspicions end? God, this was awful.

And yet, it wasn't, too, I thought, as I resumed my place at my usual chair, and unfolded my laptop. Alexandra had given my niece a new lease of life, by leaving me that much money. Granted, it would take another few months to come through, so if Gabby could just hang on till then...

Even so, I'd taken Alexandra's words very seriously. She'd told me to look for Archie's buried goods, and I now intended to. Until I'd read her letter today, I'd taken the notion of searching for the buried treasure with a pinch of salt. It seemed like a childish whim until then, a silly fantasy. But reading her letter after her death made me see the whole thing in a different light. Alexandra had been killed – and the most likely motive was money. The legend of Archie's buried treasure probably played its part in this. But it was like Alexandra had been speaking to me from beyond her grave. She'd had such a hunch that she was going to die – because of murder – that she'd taken steps to look after me after she was gone. I still didn't know what dark secrets most of the family members were hiding, other than what Jesse had told me, and I had no idea about the staff – although I had to admit that Mr Brentwood had been looking at me strangely recently. But I was most determinedly on Alexandra's side with all this. And if I could find the buried goods, then there would be an excellent chance that I could send Gabby to America very soon...

I'd already decided that Alexandra's death wouldn't be in vain, I reflected, standing up to peruse the shelves once more. That I would do my best to uncover the truth while trying to raise money for Gabby. But what I'd found out today with Mr Murphy had transformed my views further. Alexandra had really gone out of her way to look after me. She didn't know me personally, but out of justice to Beatrice and Jacob, she'd decided to give me a piece of her inheritance. And more than that, she'd told me to find the treasure, and reiterated the view that she'd like me to discover it, rather than any of her other relatives. I wasn't sure why she felt like she did about them, but it didn't matter. By leaving me the money, she had quite probably saved my niece's life. As a thank you, I was determined to honour her wishes and to get to the bottom of the *rot* at Godwyne, as she called it. And if she wanted me to look for Archie's treasure, I thought, as I grabbed some very specific files, then I was as sure as hell going to do that too. And I had an idea about where to start...

Research, Alexandra had told me in both her notes – the one left in my laptop and the one Mr Murphy had given me – was the key to solving this awful mystery. And if I was good at one thing in life, it was just that. The killer may be several steps ahead of me at the moment, but they didn't have the years of experience that I did; the hours, days and weeks spent studying documents, the different courses I'd been on, the books I'd written. Research was where my advantage lay, I realised, and I fully intended to put it to good use.

I opened the top file, and got back to work...

Chapter Twenty-Eight

After two hours of hard study, I'd unearthed a lot of information. But it didn't tell me anything new, just confirmed what I'd already found out. Archie's increasing frustration at his wife's lack of care about the repairs and upkeep at Godwyne, her rampant social life, her horrid treatment of their daughter Beatrice and obvious favour of Ottilie. Her lack of interest in his hobbies, namely archaeology, and how she constantly berated him about spending so much time out of the house. Beatrice's wedding day – a very low-key affair compared with Ottilie's by all accounts – and Cordelia's apparent dislike of Beatrice's new husband, John.

I stood up, feeling frustrated. From what Alexandra had implied, there was much more information to be found in here, things I hadn't already stumbled upon. There was no point repeatedly confirming what I already knew, I had to find fresh information. I just wasn't sure where to look. Then a thought struck me. What if it wasn't on display on the shelves, like all the journals and letters I'd already looked through? What if someone – maybe Archie or Alexandra – had hidden it away somewhere, so that the documents remained safe from people with bad intentions?

I began rooting around the room, looking for anywhere that might hold papers. Behind rows of books, in any drawers and cupboards I could find, under the enormous rug. I even inspected the floorboards to see if any were loose. *Oh God,* I thought, sitting back on my heels. *I hope Archie hasn't put them in the wrong file to confuse people. It will take me months to find them if that's the case...*

Standing up, feeling rather despondent, I looked around the library again. *If I was Archie,* I thought, *where would I hide secret documents? What would I think would be the most unlikely place anyone would look?*

Slowly – a brainwave hitting me – I turned towards the musty old display cabinet that held many of Archie's finds. It clearly hadn't been touched for years. As I walked towards it, peering inside, I saw that several centimetres of dust had collected on top of each item. Archie had been right when he wrote in his diary that no one was interested in his archaeological treasures. His family hadn't been in the early twentieth century, and his descendants weren't now. Except for me...

I brushed the cobwebs away from the latch on the glass door, and turned the small handle. It opened. It smelt musty, and made me feel as though I was going to sneeze. I stared at the artefacts inside, wondering which one might hold some secrets. I picked up a chipped brown pot and stared inside. It was empty, bar layers of dust. I put it back, and picked up what looked like some sort of broken religious relic. It was rectangular and had a carved cross on its front. *Archie must have found it when he was searching among monastery ruins,* I thought, turning it over in my hands. No papers hidden there. Most of the other things in the cabinet were too small to hold any documents; shallow pots, miniature bowls, old coins, bones, stones and what looked like a faded piece of mosaic. There was a skull at the back of the second shelf, and while I'd never been keen on looking at human anatomy – I'd fainted in a science class when I was younger when the teacher made us dissect a pig's heart – I made myself reach forward and pick it up. I turned it over. That's when I saw the bundle of documents, wrapped in string, and stuffed up inside the frontal lobe.

Chapter Twenty-Nine

All squeamish thoughts immediately forgotten, I retrieved the yellowing papers with shaking hands, and placed the skull back in the cabinet, shutting the door. I took the documents back to my desk, and spread them out, studying them. On first glance, they all appeared to be letters. I picked up one and started to read.

Dear Charles, it began. *Now that name sounds familiar*, I thought, opening my notebook. *Ah yes, Charles Fitzconner had been Archie's friend, the one who owned successful mines.*

I did appreciate your reply to my last note. No, sadly nothing has improved here at Godwyne. If anything, the situation has worsened. I am at a loss to know what to do. Cordy's treatment of Beatie is unbearably cruel. She seems determined to banish the poor girl, and all because of her condition. Now that Ottilie has a son, Cordy cannot bear to think that young Jacob – who she thinks may have inherited Beatrice's sickness

– will one day be Lord of Godwyne. I cannot see anything wrong with this myself, he is a wonderful child and quite healthy. But Cordy has started such intrigue and meddling that it makes my stomach turn. And to think, poor Beatie is with child again...

What? I thought, putting the letter down. *Beatrice had a second child?* Now this was a surprise. I was sure that Alexandra hadn't mentioned this fact. Perhaps the younger child didn't survive? Maybe that was why? Because as far as I knew, Beatrice had only had one son – Jacob. Or perhaps Alexandra's eyesight had failed before she found out this detail...

I picked up another letter.

My Dearest Charles, Archie had written:

I'm afraid desperate measures are now needed. It pains me more than I can say, but Cordy has concocted a terrible plan to remove Beatie from the Trengrouse line. I have done everything in my power to try and stop this from happening, but to no avail. Cordy has gone too far, and Beatie and John are now removed from the home...

Gosh, this was terrible, I thought. It was so sad. And to think that Archie had really loved his daughter, but had been unable to stop the calamitous series of events from happening...

I continued reading.

My wife and I no longer speak. It is like we are

strangers now. But Cordy's only care is for Ottilie and Francis. Beatie must have had the baby by now, but I am in doubt as to whether I will ever meet the little thing as I have no idea where they are now living...

I picked up another letter.

My state of health has worsened, old boy, and I am afraid that I won't last too much longer. Not that I will be sorry to go. Life is more painful than I can bear nowadays. My wife constantly tells me that I spend far too much time excavating old rubbish, and so accordingly I spend as much time as possible doing just that. Cordy and Ottilie continue to ruin themselves and the family, and so I have taken action. I have collected the valuables from the castle and have buried them in the site I took you to last. The dug-out one. Beatie is gone, and I have no wish to let any of the survivors wreak havoc on what is left of the Trengrouse fortune. No doubt they would simply sell anything of value in order to pay for another party, and I just will not be party to that sort of senseless extravagance. Please keep this information private, old thing, as my wife and daughter need to learn a lesson about waste and greed. As far as I am concerned, the valuables can stay hidden until a worthy member of the family has enough common sense to find them. If they possess that, then they clearly deserve the items...

Wow, I thought, lowering the paper. So it was true. Archie really did bury several bits of Trengrouse treasure. In the site that he last showed Charles. Where on earth could that be? What did he mean by 'the dug-out one'? Surely all his excavations were dug out? There must be a lot more to the grounds than I realised. Maybe Jesse would know what this means? He's probably more acquainted with the land and buildings on the estate than anyone else. Maybe even more than the family.

A noise behind me made me jump. I looked round, and saw the door handle turning...

Chapter Thirty

Jesse's tanned face appeared at the door.

'Oh, it's you,' I said, exhaling. 'I was just thinking that you might be able to help me with something I've found.'

'Just came to check up on how you're doing,' Jesse said, coming in. 'I'm on a break for fifteen minutes, so I was wondering if you wanted me to help you move your stuff to my house?'

'Good idea,' I said, closing my laptop and standing up. My eyes flickered automatically to the camera on the ceiling; I was sure no one could see me at my desk. The idea of being watched while I worked was so creepy. 'Not that I have many things here at all, but given everything that's happened, it would be good to have some company. To be honest, I'm a bit worried about going up to my room by myself. Someone might have been in there again while I've been here, and I can't bear the thought of receiving another one of those creepy notes.'

'You okay about working in the library though?' Jesse said, as I put my laptop and other bits into my bag before stuffing the letters back into the skull in the cabinet, with Jesse's expression becoming incredulous as he watched. 'I mean, I don't know how safe it is for you to be in here by yourself, Grace. There are video cameras everywhere, but what if Mr Brentwood and Zara miss something?'

'No, not really.' I managed a small smile. 'I'm not that keen on being here on my own, if truth be told. I'm pretty terrified the whole time now. But I know you're busy, I can't ask you to be my minder all the time. And I need to get this research done. It's so important, and it's up to me to do it – no one else. I've found out quite a lot today already, and I need to tell you about the hidden letters...'

As we made our way out of the library and through the labyrinthine corridors, I filled Jesse in on how I'd discovered Archie's hidden letters in the skull, and what they'd said about the 'dug-out' place. We'd just got to the stone staircase that led up to the staff rooms, when we heard raised voices coming from somewhere nearby. Jesse stopped and turned to me, his finger on his lips. We stopped walking and became very still.

'No, I'm sorry, Derek, but things have gone too far now,' Mrs Taylor was saying. She sounded upset. 'It's time for me to say what I know.'

'Absolutely not, Margaret.' Mr Brentwood was almost shouting. 'I will not have you dragging the family's name through the mud. Think of what's at stake.'

'Lives are at stake, Derek.' Mrs Taylor sounded close to tears now. 'Can't you see that? I couldn't live with myself if anything else awful happened.'

'Nothing else is going to happen,' Mr Brentwood said, his tone furious. 'Lady Trengrouse's death was an accident. It has been officially ruled as such, and you'll just have to accept it.'

'No, Derek,' Mrs Taylor said in a small voice. 'We both know that it wasn't.'

'Oh for God's sake,' Mr Brentwood said loudly. Then there was a thump, as though he'd hit a table with his fist. 'I won't have you doing this, Margaret. Not on my watch. The damage would be irreparable.'

'The damage has already been done,' Mrs Taylor said with a sob.

Chapter Thirty One

Footsteps could be heard in the room. They sounded like they were getting closer to us. Someone was going to open the door at any moment...

'We have to go,' I hissed to Jesse, and we both ran up the stairs as quietly as we could. A door opened behind us, but we were just out of sight. We got to my room, piled in, and closed the door.

'What the hell was all that about?' I whispered.

Jesse sat down on the bed, looking pale.

'I'm not sure,' he said, shaking his head. 'But I've thought for a while that Derek is receiving extra pay from a Trengrouse, probably Edward, to help minimise any scandal that goes on here at Godwyne.'

'What do you mean?' I said, as I opened a drawer and began bundling clothes into my bag.

'I mean that if anything happens here at the castle,' Jesse said slowly, 'no one ever gets to hear about it. It's like it gets erased from everyone's memories. Like the time when Will got drunk and crashed his car into a visitor's vehicle so hard that it had to be written off. Both cars were removed from the drive within an hour, the visitor left the castle – probably with a big payout – and nothing was ever mentioned about it again. And the time when Helena was having an affair with a married diplomat in London. There was one small article about it in the *Daily Mail*, then Mr Brentwood became very busy for a few days and then there was nothing more about it in the papers ever again. And it was never talked about here, apart from among the staff when Mrs Taylor wasn't listening.'

'Hmm,' I said, hoisting the bag onto my shoulder. 'So you think that even if Mrs Taylor and Mr Brentwood have proof that someone killed Alexandra, he is now on damage control for appearance's sake, and won't let the truth come out?'

'Yep,' Jesse said, standing up. 'Exactly. Right, have you got all your things?'

I nodded.

'Then let's go to my cottage and I'll show you your new room,' he said, with a kind smile.

We'd made our way down to the main hall, when Mrs Taylor came running towards me, Hobnob walking fast behind her, meowing.

'Oh, Grace,' she said. 'There you are. I've been looking everywhere for you.' Her eyes were red.

'Is everything all right, Mrs Taylor?' I said.

'I need to talk to you,' Mrs Taylor said. 'It's urgent. Have you got five minutes to spare, dear? And do call me Margaret, won't you? I know we've only known each other for a few days but Mrs Taylor sounds far too formal now.'

'Ah, yes of course,' I said, looking at Jesse, doubting that I'd ever be able to call her Margaret. It was like a teacher asking you to call them by their first name. 'I'll just be a couple of minutes, er, Margaret. I just have to drop something off somewhere while Jesse is on his break, and then I'll be right back. Is that okay? I won't be long at all.' I knew Jesse didn't have much time to spare, and it seemed rude to keep him waiting when he'd opened his house to me.

'Yes, dear,' Mrs Taylor looked around, her eyes wide, 'I'll wait for you here.'

'Let's walk quickly,' I said to Jesse, as we trotted down the front steps. 'Mrs Taylor looks really upset. I want to get back to her as soon as I can.'

It didn't take long to get to Jesse's cottage. He showed me upstairs to a small but perfectly lovely little room with white walls and sparse but attractive furniture. Dumping my clothes on top of the pale-blue duvet, I grabbed my laptop and handbag, and said goodbye to Jesse, who explained he had to go and spray the weeds on the other side of the estate.

'I'll come back and check on you again in a bit,' he called after me as I set off back up the path. 'I think someone's been out digging again. God knows who it is, I'm going to try and find out who – make sure it's not some of the village boys sneaking onto the estate again.'

'Thank you,' I called over my shoulder. It was a great feeling to have him looking out for me during my stay at Godwyne, it made me feel a tiny bit safer. Although my stomach was now in knots again, wondering what on earth Mrs Taylor – or Margaret – was going to say...

It was then that I saw Hobnob belting away from the castle, her eyes wide and her ears flat against her head. Something must have freaked her out, I thought. She normally seemed like such a calm cat.

I jumped up the stone stairs two at a time, and pushed open the big front door. Then stopped.

Mrs Taylor was lying on the marble floor, blood oozing from a wound in her head.

Chapter Thirty-Two

'Oh Christ,' I whispered, taking my phone out of my pocket, my hands shaking. I knelt down next to her head, punching in three nines.

'Ambulance,' I said as soon as the emergency services operator answered. 'I need an ambulance immediately at Godwyne Castle. And police too. Someone's been attacked.'

Mrs Taylor made a gurgling sound.

'She's still alive,' I told the man on the end of the phone. 'Come quickly, please.'

I stared in anguish at poor Mrs Taylor, desperately wanting to help her in some way but not knowing whether I'd make her condition worse by touching her. Should I put her in the recovery position? No, I thought. Not with that head injury. Best leave her as she was and hope that the paramedics arrived extremely quickly. They'd be the best people to help her.

Mr Brentwod and Zara appeared at the door to the office. Zara gave a small cry and her hands went to her mouth. Mr Brentwood's eyes widened.

I glared at him. After what I'd heard him saying to Mrs Taylor earlier, I strongly suspected that he was behind this attack, and planned to tell the police exactly what I knew. Why else would he have tried to silence the poor woman? If he was just an innocent member of staff, then surely he would have supported Mrs Taylor in her wish to tell the police about what she'd overheard the night before. There was minimising scandal, and then there was withholding evidence, and I sure as hell knew which one I suspected he was doing...

I looked back at poor Mrs Taylor, and although she seemed unconscious – barely clinging to life – I told her softly that the paramedics were on their way and that everything was going to be fine, just in case she could hear me. I wanted to hold her hand, do something that might comfort her. But I was scared to touch her in any way, just in case I did more harm than good.

Shortly after that, everything became a blur of activity. Sirens heralded the arrival of the paramedics and police, and seconds after they arrived the entrance hall was full of medic and police neon jackets. After the paramedics had initially tended to Mrs Taylor, they brought a stretcher in, and carefully loaded her onto it.

Just as they were wheeling it towards the door, Helena arrived.

'Oh God,' she said, her voice a wail. 'What's going on?' She stared at Mrs Taylor. 'Why is she like that? Has she been hurt?'

'She has, and she's in a critical condition,' one of the paramedics said. 'We need to get her to the hospital as soon as we can. Can you move please so that we can get past?'

Helena seemed rooted to the spot, she didn't move at all, so I leaned over, grabbed her arm, and dragged her out of the way. It didn't take much effort, she was a skinny thing, and was soon standing at the side next to me.

As Mrs Taylor was being loaded into the ambulance, the rest of the family – who Mr Brentwood must have phoned – arrived en masse.

'What's going on?' Edward said as he ran up the stone steps towards us. 'We came as soon as Derek called. What exactly has been going on here?'

'Someone attacked Mrs Taylor,' I said, staring at Mr Brentwood. 'She's been hit on the head so hard that she's barely alive.' *Try and call* this *incident an accident*, I thought, my blood boiling with anger and grief.

Sukie, heading up the steps behind her husband, put her hand on her mouth, her eyes wide.

'Someone's attacked Margaret?' Will said, his voice a boom, as he pushed past his mother and father. 'Well we don't have to look very far to find the perpetrator, do we?' He stopped and turned towards me. 'Everything at Godwyne has gone wrong since you arrived, Grace the Writer.'

'That is *enough*, Will,' Howard said, coming to stand next to his brother, his wife Mimi close behind, shock on her face. 'No one needs to be accused by us at the moment. We need to let the police do their job, and properly investigate this crime.'

A plain-clothes officer stepped out of the castle and joined our large throng. He was stocky, like a rugby player, and had the stony gaze of a man who'd become immune to murderous situations.

'Lord Trengrouse,' he said to Edward. 'I'm Detective Inspector Paynter. We are going to need to interview everybody who was on the estate today. No one is to leave until we have finished speaking to every last member of the family and each person who is on the staff. Also any visitors who happened to be in or around the castle at the time. Can you assign us some private rooms where we can conduct these interviews please?'

'Yes, of course.' Edward nodded, his face grim. 'Follow me, Detective.'

Will watched his father and the detective head into the castle, and then turned to me.

'One guess as to who I'm going to say I think the attacker is,' he said to me, his tone vicious.

But I didn't care. I was too busy watching Mr Brentwood. He'd gone very pale, and was muttering something to Zara, several feet away from the rest of us. I certainly planned to tell the detective everything that I'd overheard him saying to Mrs Taylor. Because – although Will was clearly keen to put the blame on me – as far as I could see, Mr Brentwood was the only viable suspect right now...

Chapter Thirty-Three

I was sitting in the staff dining hall, watching Mary place a steaming mug of tea in front of me. It was just the two of us in there; Jesse had come running over as soon as word reached him about what had happened to Mrs Taylor. With tears in his eyes, he'd asked me to tell him about it. Then a police officer had arrived and told him that it was his turn to be interviewed. I was filled with a cold fear now, worried that all the family members – based on Will's words – would point the finger of suspicion at me, and that the police would take them seriously and that I'd become their number one suspect. After all, it had been me who'd found Mrs Taylor lying on the floor, hadn't it? I was terrified that they'd somehow convince the police that I'd done it.

I'd already been questioned, and had told the poker-faced Detective Paynter about overhearing the two conversations between Mrs Taylor and Mr Brentwood. How in the first, on the night of Alexandra's death, Mrs Taylor had said she'd overheard two people saying that something needed to be done soon. And how Mr Brentwood had told her that she must say nothing to anyone about it. Then, how today Jesse and I had heard them talking – or shouting – again, with Mrs Taylor saying that it was time to tell what she knew, and Mr Brentwood telling her again that she must do no such thing. How he'd insisted that Lady Trengrouse's death had been an accident, and how Mrs Taylor – very upset – had then said that they both knew it wasn't. Then how Mrs Taylor had found me as I was on my way to Jesse's house to leave my belongings there, and how she'd said she needed to talk to me urgently.

'And I was as quick as I could be,' I told Detective Paynter. 'I literally dumped my stuff and ran back to the castle. But she'd already been attacked.'

The detective had regarded me quietly, his face giving away nothing.

'So you were the one who first discovered that Margaret Taylor had been attacked,' he said. 'That's interesting. Especially seeing as you were so new to the castle. What bad luck to have that happen so shortly after your arrival. And may I ask why were you moving your belongings into Mr Benson's cottage, Miss Haythorpe, when I understand that you had already been allocated a room in the staff quarters?'

So I explained to him about how I didn't believe that Alexandra's death was an accident, whatever the ruling, told him all about what she'd said to me about being directly related to Archie – went into the whole family connection with Beatrice and Jacob and everything, and the coincidence with the epilepsy. The fact that I'd heard footsteps running away after our conversation ended, how someone had obviously been listening. How Will had been so rude to me since I arrived at Godwyne, and that Sukie hadn't been all that pleasant either. In fact, how each and every one of the Trengrouses seemed to have motives that may spur them on to protect family money. How – on Alexandra's instructions – I was planning to go and visit her the night she'd died, as she wanted to give me the birth and marriage certificates, but then how I'd fallen asleep, tired after a busy day, only to be awoken by Mimi's scream. How I'd seen Alexandra dead outside on the gravel.

'And you didn't think to tell the police any of this directly after the incident?' Detective Paynter said. 'You didn't think that this might be a very valuable piece of knowledge for us to have?'

'Well everyone was saying that they thought her death was an accident,' I said. *Shit,* I was thinking. *Does he actually suppose I might be a suspect here? What has everyone else been saying about me? This is beyond ridiculous. I'm the one suspecting everyone else, but Will thinks it's me behind all this.* 'I didn't think the police would take it seriously, as I had no evidence to prove that she was pushed out of a window.'

'Hmm.' Detective Paynter's eyes had narrowed. He'd ended the interview soon after that point.

Mary placed her mug on the table and sat down opposite me. Her eyes were grave.

'Listen, love,' she said. 'I think there's a few things that I need to tell you.'

I looked at her. Tried to focus. My thoughts felt like they were splintering. I couldn't believe I'd been so stupid, that I hadn't gone to the police the day after Alexandra was found dead – not that the family had either. Or given them the letters. I should have told them everything then. If only I'd said something at the time then Mrs Taylor might not have been attacked today. If I hadn't been so intent on finding out about my birthright... Oh God, why the hell did I ever come to Godwyne Castle?

'Yes?' I said.

Mary sighed.

'Margaret and I are old friends,' she said, wrapping her hands around her mug. 'We've worked together long enough. Our lives have always been here at Godwyne. And we may bicker sometimes – what friends don't? And she usually doesn't like me speaking my mind about the family. She's always been much more straight and upright in her manners than me. But we've always been close too. And Margaret has told me a few things since Lady Trengrouse met her death. She came to see me about an hour before you found her lying there, in fact. And I almost fell off my chair when I heard what she had to say.'

'Christ,' I said. 'What did she say?'

'That she had to tell someone what was eating her up inside,' Mary said. 'She told me that she believed that Lady Trengrouse had been murdered. That she'd overheard a conversation between two people, the night before her body was found, and that one was saying to the other that something had to be done soon.'

I nodded. I couldn't tell Mary that I'd overheard that very same conversation, as it would sound like I was a snoopy eavesdropper, and enough suspicion was already on me.

'Wow,' I said. 'Do you know, Mary, I also think that Lady Trengrouse was killed by someone.'

I explained that Alexandra had entrusted me with some very sensitive information the previous day after dinner, and that someone had been listening to us. That Alexandra had told me to come and see her that night, and the next thing I knew was that she was dead.

Mary nodded, tears in her eyes.

'Look, love,' she said. 'I should probably tell you that Margaret told me about you being directly related to old Lord Archie.'

'She knew?' I said, feeling my eyes grow wide.

'Yes, she knew,' Mary said. She sighed. 'The thing you have to understand, Grace, is that for us older staff who've worked here at Godwyne for decades, this place is our home. We feel protective over it. I might grumble about the Trengrouse family – goodness knows they are hard work – but in a way their secrets are our secrets. And we know most of what goes on. The family never stop talking when I wheel their food into the dining room. I hear some very interesting things. And so does Margaret. But we never say anything about the important stuff. We keep it under our hats, if you know what I mean?'

I nodded.

'I wasn't aware of your close connection to the Trengrouses until Margaret told me today,' Mary went on. 'But I knew about Beatrice and her son Jacob, and how they'd been disinherited by Cordelia, all those years ago. Heard the family discussing it many times. I thought you might find out about it, if you were good enough at your research. But I had no idea that it would affect you so personally.'

'It makes sense that you both know a lot about what goes on here,' I said. 'And I suppose Margaret is probably involved most of all with the family.'

'She is,' Mary said, taking a sip of tea. 'Margaret told me today that she feels that very bad business is afoot, here at the castle. She said that she wanted to tell the police about the overheard conversation, but that Derek wouldn't let her.'

I nodded.

'She said she felt that all of this might have something to do with you,' Mary said. 'I'm sorry to tell you this, love, but she said she thinks your life might be in danger. That you should leave Godwyne for your own safety. She started mumbling a bit after that, so I couldn't understand everything she was saying, but it seemed to be something to do with Jacob's descendants. That there's more than just you, and she thinks that the family are determined to stop you and your sister, or the other child making any claim on the inheritance.'

I stared at her.

'Other child?' I said. *Does she mean Gabby?* I thought.

'Yes, dear,' Mary said. 'The one that's descended from Beatrice's daughter, Emilia. If the family acted all surprised about finding out that you were a direct descendant of Jacob's, then I'm afraid it was all theatricals on their part. They're not stupid, they've kept an eye on his descendants for years. They are only interested in protecting their money, you see. And don't want any outsiders turning up to dilute it.'

'Shit,' I said. 'Do you really think one of the Trengrouses would go as far as to kill, just for money?'

'Of course they would,' Mary said. 'Even I knew that Jacob had descendants, although when you first arrived I didn't know you were one of them. It's common knowledge among some of the staff here. Adds to the mystery of the place, I suppose. And don't forget, dear, that money is the motive behind many crimes.'

'Who is Jacob's daughter's descendant?' I said, my mind blown by this news.

'Now that I don't know,' Mary said. And as I stared into her eyes, I thought she was telling the truth. 'But you see, Grace, Margaret had become very worried about your safety here. She ummed and ahhed about telling you anything, such was her loyalty to the family. But when Lady Trengrouse was killed, she got to thinking, and started putting two and two together. And she realised that it was probably more than a coincidence that her death happened just after you'd arrived here.'

'Oh God,' I said. I already knew that I was in danger, but hearing Mary say it made it all the more real. I could feel an icy chill spreading throughout my body. I looked around, half expecting a killer to emerge from somewhere in the room. 'Well,

Jesse has said I can stay in his spare room while I'm here, so I think I'll be safer there.'

'Maybe.' Mary looked at me, her expression quizzical. 'But why don't you just leave now, while you have the chance? You've been left an inheritance by Lady Trengrouse...'

'You know about that too?' I cut across her words, but I couldn't help it.

'Like I told you, dear,' Mary said with a small smile, 'Margaret and I get to hear about pretty much everything at Godwyne, one way or another.'

'The thing is,' I said, 'I can't go yet. I promised Alexandra – I mean Lady Trengrouse – that I would do something before I left. And my niece, Gabby, is so ill. I need to raise the money to get her to America for treatment. And right now, I'm prepared to risk my own life to do that.'

Mary studied me for a moment.

'Then be very, very careful, Grace,' she said. 'Because...'

A noise behind me made us both jump. I turned to see Mr Brentwood coming into the room.

Chapter Thirty-Four

'Ah, Mary,' Mr Brentwood said. 'The detective would like to see you now.'

I stood up at the same time as Mary, who was now muttering something about not being able to find Hobnob anywhere, and followed her out of the dining room. There was no way I wanted to be left in the same room as that man. I had no idea about what he might do or say to me. My head was reeling. So there was another descendant of Jacob's who was also entitled to their share of the inheritance? I wondered if they knew about the crazy, landed family of which they were a part of, or if the news would come as a total shock once they were found and told. So Beatrice's daughter, Emilie, had survived. I couldn't help wondering why Alexandra hadn't told me about her. Maybe she didn't know?

I wanted to find Jesse, as I'd had an idea, and needed his help. Rain clouds were gathering overhead as I walked through the early evening greying light, wondering where he could be.

Could Mr Brentwood really be behind all this? I wondered, rounding the side of the castle and setting out towards the sound of a power tool. What on earth would his motive be? Jesse said that he acts as some sort of scandal-limiter for the family, so maybe he gets a lot of extra money for doing that. Perhaps he's even more wedded to his job than Mrs Taylor or Mary, and is prepared to do absolutely anything in order to protect the Trengrouses?

Or, I thought, heading towards some trees – the sound seemed to be coming from beyond them – maybe I've jumped to conclusions, and it's a member of the Trengrouse family behind all this after all. I mean, that would make more sense. And Will has been the most ghastly to me since I arrived. But he just seems too obvious? *Oh, I don't know...*

Pushing through the leaves, I stepped out onto a large flat piece of grass. Jesse was standing about two hundred metres away, ear defenders on, strimming weeds along the edge of the grass. Zara was walking towards him, and from the way she was waving her arms, looked like she was trying to get his attention. She always looked so smart, I thought. So professionally dressed. She was the person I'd spoken to least since arriving at Godwyne, although she'd always shown a keen interest in everything I'd told the staff in the dining room, bless her.

I watched, as Jesse saw her, lowered the strimmer and took his ear defenders off. Zara handed him something, and after a brief conversation, turned and walked away.

I shouted to him as I walked over. He turned, and waved something in the air. As I got closer, I could see that it was an envelope.

'What's that?' I said, arriving next to him.

'It's for you,' Jesse said. 'Zara said she's been trying to find you, but couldn't, so she came to give it to me to pass on. She said it arrived on her desk a little while ago.'

My skin went cold as I looked at the writing. I immediately knew where I'd seen it before.

Ripping open the envelope, I unfolded the white paper. We both stared at it.

> *GRACE. GO HOME. I'VE WARNED YOU BEFORE. IF YOU DON'T, THEN EXPECT THE END TO COME TONIGHT.*

Chapter Thirty-Five

'Fuck.' Jesse's eyes were scared-looking. 'We need to take this straight to that detective.'

I nodded. I felt sick. I was scared shitless now. Whoever it was behind all this just wasn't going to give up. And Mary was right, everything that had happened at Godwyne was about me. I couldn't stay there any longer, couldn't risk someone else – or me – getting killed. It was all very well saying that I was willing to risk my life, but when it came down to it, what was the point of that? Who would it help, if I was murdered, if I hadn't managed to raise any immediate funds? If Gabby needed to get her treatment before my inheritance from Alexandra came through, then I'd just have to find another way to get the money. Things had gone far enough.

'Yep,' I said, the paper in my hands shaking. 'And then can you walk me back to your house, Jesse? I need to pack up and leave now. Things have gone too far. Whoever the sick person is that's behind all this is obviously not going to give up unless I'm either dead or out of the way somehow. So I need to go back to London. I can see that now. I probably should have gone days ago, and then Mrs Taylor might not have been attacked. I can't stay and risk anything else happening.'

A mixture of emotions fluttered over Jesse's face; disappointment, sadness, understanding.

'Okay,' he said. 'I think you're right, Grace. It's too dangerous for you to stay here now. But hopefully we can stay in touch? I've really enjoyed getting to know you.'

'I'd like that,' I said, as we walked fast towards the castle. Meeting Jesse had been the one bright spot in the whole dark affair of Godwyne – other than Alexandra's kind bequeath, of course. If circumstances had been different, I would most definitely have stayed on to get to know him better. I was starting to really like him, in a deep kind of way. He was so kind and caring, so straightforward. And really attractive, in an outdoor bronzed kind of way. But life clearly had other ideas, and I had to get away before any other attacks took place. I had no real idea who was behind the carnage at Godwyne, but whoever it was clearly had it in for me. And I was out of energy and bravado now, I just wanted to get the hell away from this grey stone nightmare of a place.

We walked on in silence, both deep in thought. As we neared the castle walls, Jesse looked up.

'Just making sure that no one's up there ready to push any more statues down on you,' he said with a grimace.

'Thank you for looking after me,' I said, meaning it.

He took my hand and squeezed it.

We entered the big entrance hall, to find Mr Brentwood standing there, his face pale.

'Where's the detective?' Jesse said. 'We need to speak to him.'

'He's just left,' Mr Brentwood said in a dazed way. 'All the police have gone now. Detective Paynter said he'd be back first thing tomorrow to continue the investigation.'

'Have they taken anyone with them?' Jesse said. 'Has anyone been arrested?'

'Not to my knowledge,' Mr Brentwood said.

Jesse's gaze caught mine.

'Come with me,' he said, heading back towards the front door.

'I didn't want to say anything else in front of Derek,' he whispered, as we walked down the steps. 'I don't know who to trust here anymore.'

'Especially after what he said to Mrs Taylor earlier,' I muttered back. 'I told the police about that.'

'So did I,' Jesse said, his face grim. 'Maybe they questioned Derek about it. Perhaps that's why he looks like he's just been hit over the head with something.'

'Wait,' I said, stopping. 'I've got an idea. Can you come to the Upper Library with me quickly? If I'm leaving Godwyne, I'd like to take some documents with me so that I can continue the research in London. I still want to honour Alexandra's wishes and get to the bottom of what's happening, and who I really am. I can still do that remotely, I don't have to be on site to continue looking through everything.'

'Okay,' Jesse said, turning round. 'But we better do it quickly. I don't want to be in that building for very long. It's not safe in there now. We can drive down to the police station and show the detective the letter after that, before you set off home.'

Minutes later, we'd walked back through the entrance hall – now empty – and made our way up to the library.

Going straight to the cabinet, I opened the door and picked up the skull, turning it upside down.

The letters were gone. The skull was completely empty.

'No,' I mumbled, putting it back, and searching through the cabinet. 'No, this can't be happening.' I looked in the pot, underneath everything, behind the cabinet. I went back to the desk, looking all around that in case I'd forgotten to put the letters in the cabinet – so much had happened and although I was sure I had replaced the letters my head was full of confusion.

'They've gone,' I said, turning to Jesse. And then a thought hit me.

Only Jesse knew that I'd found Archie's secret documents; he'd been with me in the library earlier, come to find me to ask if I wanted to take my belongings to his cottage. It felt like the bottom was falling out of my world. No one else could have known they were there.

I stared at him.

'Where are they, Jesse?' I said.

'What?' he said, his brow crinkling. 'I have no idea, Grace. Why would I know? I remember seeing you put them in the skull before we went up to your room. That's the last time I saw them.'

'But you are the only other person – apart from me – who knows that they exist,' I said, feeling tears spring to my eyes. 'And where they were kept. And now they're gone.'

Jesse's mouth opened. Then it shut again. He didn't seem to know what to say.

'Do you really not trust me, Grace?' he said eventually, his eyes full of hurt. 'After everything I've done to try and look after you?'

I paused. He wasn't the only one filled with hurt. I had trusted him, told him everything I knew. But now my head was spinning, and nothing made sense. I didn't know why he would have taken Archie's letters, but it was the only possible thing that could have happened.

I gave a small shrug.

'I don't know,' I said, my voice faint. 'I don't know anything anymore.'

Jesse shook his head.

'I've got nothing to do with any of this, Grace,' he said. 'If you can't see that, then I don't know what to tell you. I've tried to look after you, tried to help you in any way that I can. But if you still suspect me after all that, then I don't know what to do.'

For a moment, it looked like he was going to say more. But then he sighed, turned, and walked out of the library.

I stood there for a moment, watching the door close.

Fuck, I thought. *Maybe I'm wrong. I hope I am. But who else could have taken the letters?*

I knelt down, and inspected each and every item in the cabinet again, just in case I'd been mistaken and had accidentally put the letters back in a different object earlier. They definitely weren't on the top of the second shelf, I established. I bent down further, and inspected the super-dusty lowest shelf. The artefacts on this one were all quite small, there was no way any of them could be hiding any documents. But in my desperation, I looked through them anyway, picking up a coin, then a brooch, then an old mug. Which rattled.

I turned it upside down, and an old key – covered in rust – fell out on to my hand.

Just then, a whirring noise came from the ceiling.

I looked up, and saw the camera lens getting bigger. It was pointing straight at me.

Chapter Thirty Six

Of course, I thought, standing up, clutching the key. I'd been so stupid. Anyone looking at the CCTV footage could have seen me finding Archie's letters in the skull. Anyone in the office can see what's going on, and the family all have access to the video at all times. Someone was probably watching me right now. After moving my desk out of the camera's view, I'd felt safe in the library, sure that no one could see what I was doing. But in fact, the camera would still be able to take in the view of the cabinet. Why hadn't I thought of that before? Right, I had to go and find Jesse and apologise. Explain that I'd had a moment of madness when I'd accused him of taking the letters. And show him the key. Did it signal that we were a step closer to finding Archie's buried hoard? I didn't know how, but Jesse might have some ideas...

Grabbing my bags, I headed out of the library and towards the nearest set of stairs. I was gutted that the letters had gone, but now that I'd remembered about the camera, I wasn't surprised. There was a very bad person – or people – on the loose at Godwyne, and they weren't stupid. They wanted to eliminate any trace of my connection with Archie, and any lead

I had on the buried valuables. And they'd succeeded in making me leave the estate and go back to London. Once I'd found Jesse, and shown him the key, and profusely apologised for accusing him, I'd go and get my belongings and head off back to my home. Penny would be pleased when I told her about our inheritance, and if Gabby needed to get to America soon then I'd find a way to help her do that somehow...

I paused for a moment, stuffing the key into the back pocket of my jeans. It was awkward to keep carrying it when I had the two bags and was about to negotiate a steep flight of stairs.

I walked on, came to the stairwell and was about to place my foot on the top step, when I heard footsteps behind me. There was a crack, an almighty pain on the top of my head, and then the world went black...

Chapter Thirty-Seven

Pain. A slicing in my head. I tried to open my eyes, but the glimmer of light that came in hurt too much. Shutting them again, I tried to work out where I was. Lying on something cold. The floor? My head was pressing against something hard. A voice...

'Grace?' It was Jesse's voice. 'Grace? Oh my God. Please wake up.'

I mumbled something, trying to let him know that I was okay.

'What?' he said. I could feel him bending down over me, his hot breath on my face. 'What did you say, Grace?'

I groaned. And forced my eyes to open.

'Where am I?' I said, wincing at the stabbing pain each word produced in my brain.

'At the bottom of the stairs,' Jesse said. There was pure shock and horror on his face. 'I'm so sorry I left you alone in the library, Grace. It was silly of me to leave like that. I was just a bit hurt that you didn't trust me. But as I was walking away, I realised how much you're going through, and that you don't know who you can rely on here. So I came back to check you were okay, but then I heard footsteps running and when I came round the corner I found you at the bottom of the stairs.'

'It's me who needs to apologise,' I said, looking around, my vision becoming clearer. I couldn't see my laptop bag or handbag anywhere. I closed my eyes again for a moment. 'I shouldn't have accused you of taking the letters, Jesse. I realised that the camera in the library would have picked up what was going on, and that anyone could have seen me put them back in the skull. I was just coming to find you, but then I think someone hit me on the back of my head. And I think whoever it was might have stolen my bags too. That means they have my phone, my car keys, my laptop, everything.'

'Right,' Jesse said. I opened my eyes to see him pull his phone out of his pocket. 'I need to ring for an ambulance for you. And for the police. You've been attacked, Grace. We need to...'

'Hang on,' I said. 'Wait a minute.' I slowly heaved myself into a sitting position. 'I think I'm okay. I just need to sit here for a bit. Don't call anyone yet.'

'What?' Jesse said. 'Why? Seriously, Grace. You need to get that cut looked at, it's bleeding quite heavily. And the police know that Margaret was attacked here earlier. They need to hear about what's happened to you too. Whoever is doing all this needs to be caught, or none of us will be safe.'

I nodded.

'I understand,' I said. 'I will get my head looked at and tell the police. I just need to show you something first. If it's still there.'

I reached underneath myself and managed to pull the rusty key out of my back pocket.

'At least they didn't take this too,' I said, passing it to him. 'I found it in the cabinet in an old pewter mug. If someone was watching me on the CCTV they obviously thought I'd put it in one of my bags. It must have been important to Archie, as he only stored his most valuable things in that cabinet. And I think he might have left it there as a clue. Before we phone the police or anything, I just wanted to ask you if you know anywhere that the key might fit? Any old building or doors that would have been on the grounds in Archie's day? I can't help thinking that we are closer than ever to finding something that Archie hid – maybe his hoard of valuables. I just need a little more time to look into this, for Gabby's sake, before I get swamped by the emergency services again. Please. It's so important.'

Jesse stared at me for a moment, then smiled.

'You're a fighter all right, aren't you, Grace?' he said, shaking his head. 'It's one of the things I like most about you, actually. You're very stubborn too. Okay, but after we've looked into the key and where it might fit, I'm taking you to the hospital to get your head looked at, and then to the police station. We need to hand in the letter that you got earlier, and also tell them about the attack on you. Agreed?'

'Agreed,' I said with a small grin. 'Thanks, Jesse. For understanding.'

After a few more minutes, I got to my feet. I felt dizzy, but I didn't say anything to Jesse about that. I wanted to find out if the key fitted anything in the house or grounds; that was more important to me than being seen by a doctor who'd tell me that although it was bumped, bruised and cut, there was nothing he could do for my head except prescribe lots of rest. The resting could wait; I had more important things to be getting on with...

We made our way out into the castle grounds, and saw that the sky was almost dark. Jesse fished his phone out and turned on the torch.

'Okay,' I said. 'I think this key is more likely to fit into a lock somewhere in the grounds, rather than in the house. Archie was an outside man, he loved excavating and digging – and also burying stuff. So I think we should search out here first. Is there anywhere that you can think of that might hold a lock for this key? I've seen loads of outbuildings on the maps that are around the castle, but I have no idea where any of them are. It's best if you decide where we go first.'

'Let's think.' Jesse looked around, shining the light in front of him. 'Like you said before, it would have to be somewhere that existed back when Archie did. Lots of new outbuildings have been added since then. We could try the old stable block first? That's been there for well over a hundred years.'

He took my hand – which was nice – and led me away over the grass in a direction that I hadn't been in since arriving at the estate.

'Wait,' he said suddenly. 'Who's that?'

We stopped and stared at a shadowy figure who was walking away from the castle. Whoever it was looked fairly small and thin, and was wearing a very short skirt.

'Helena?' I said. 'What on earth is she doing sneaking about like that?'

'God knows,' Jesse said. 'She's always going off somewhere, much to Sukie's annoyance. Bleeding them dry too, with all her socialising. Maybe it's her that's doing all this to get more money? Trying to keep up a lifestyle that she can't fund herself?'

I nodded.

'Yep maybe,' I said, watching Helena disappear off into the darkness. 'I don't trust anyone here one bit now. Except you.'

Jesse gave my hand a squeeze. We walked on.

It was getting chilly, and I wrapped my free arm around myself. The air smelled sweet and fresh; the scent of freshly cut undergrowth still pervading it.

After a minute or so, I saw a dark shadowy building ahead of us over the fields.

Soon, we were outside it. As Jesse shone his torch around, I could see that it was in a ramshackle state.

'No one uses these buildings anymore,' Jesse said. 'Edward – or Lord Trengrouse should I say – has never kept horses. His father did, but he used the newer stables that were built about sixty years ago to the far left of the castle.'

We walked around the building.

'There's the door,' I said, pointing. 'It's already open.'

'Yep,' Jesse said, pushing it until we could squeeze through. 'No one comes here now. Not to my knowledge anyway. It's a pretty useless building, full of holes. Should be knocked down really. I know that at least two of the Trengrouses have done some digging round here since I've been employed at Godwyne; Edward asked me to backfill the holes. They didn't find anything, I don't think.'

Once inside the old stables, Jesse shone his torch around. There was an old tack room, six separate stables, an area that Jesse told me would have been used for feed, and another he said would have been a place where the horses were groomed. But the key fitted none of the doors, and we found no secret cupboards or trap doors or anything that it could be used for.

'Okay,' I said, turning to Jesse. 'This obviously isn't the right place. Where else do you think the key could fit? It was obviously special enough for Archie to hide it in his cabinet, not just a run-of-the-mill cupboard key or something. I can't help feeling that it fits somewhere that holds a lot of Archie's secrets.'

'Well,' Jesse said, scratching his forehead, 'there are some old monastery ruins out near the lake, to the south of the castle. Someone's been digging around there recently, but I don't know who. The family usually tell me if they're going to excavate somewhere, mostly because they want me to fill in the soil for them again afterwards. So it's a bit weird that no one has mentioned the recent mess that's been made. I mean, I see everyone wandering around in the grounds all the time. The staff as well as the family. But the recent digging is weird, especially as I have no idea who's been doing it.'

'Right,' I said, heading for the stable door, Jesse shining the torch over my head so that I could see. 'Let's go to the monastery ruins now and have a look.'

'The quickest way there,' Jesse said, once we were out in the cold night air again, 'is to cut through that copse of trees down there, and head round the lake. If we go the other way, it takes almost twice as long to get there.'

'Okay, let's take the shortcut,' I said. The cold air was making me feel better, clearing my head a bit. 'Lead the way.'

Jesse took my hand again, which I had absolutely no objections to him doing, and we set off. It was a bumpy walk, as the surface of the grass was uneven, and had patches of thistles and bracken that were hard to make out, even with the torch light.

We'd just entered the copse of trees, when we heard the sound of a car absolutely screeching down the road that led off the main drive and round the castle. It must have been about sixty metres away from where we were. Jesse immediately turned his torch light off.

'Sounds like trouble,' he said. 'And if it is, then we don't want whoever it is to know we're here.'

He wrapped his arm round me, and we both stood motionless, listening, as the car made a strange whirring noise, then ground to a halt. A door was flung open.

'You fucking idiot.' It was Sukie's voice. Her words were slurred. 'I should never have left it all to you to get on with. You've buggered this one up well and truly, like you do with everything else. And now the car has bloody broken down again. I thought you had it fixed?'

Chapter Thirty-Eight

My hand went to my mouth. I couldn't believe that I was hearing the normally super-composed ice queen speaking like this. So much for her cool, calm exterior.

Another car door opened.

'Now listen, Sukes.' It was Edward's voice. He was speaking loudly, but didn't sound as drunk as his wife. 'You just need to calm down, okay? It's probably the battery, they didn't have a new one at hand when I took the car to the garage last week. And I haven't buggered anything up. I've been working on it all day. But this kind of thing takes intelligence, judgement and good timing. Just let me get on with it in my way, all right?'

'Eddie,' Sukie said, 'we need that bloody money. Do you understand how desperate the whole thing is? We'll be absolutely fucking destitute if we don't get it. We may as well move out of Godwyne right now, the way everything is going. Do you want to save our reputation or not? Do you want to continue to mix in the circles that we do? To keep living the life that you were born into? To leave the boys with some shred of dignity when it's time for us to stop playing the game and bow out? Or do you want the world to make a mockery of us, to think that we couldn't handle ourselves, and for every bit of status we once had to die away?'

'Yes, yes.' Edward sounded frustrated. 'I know all this, Sukes, you don't have to keep reminding me. Like I said, I have it in hand. You just have to be patient for a little bit longer, all right?'

'You keep saying that, Eddie, but nothing's happening,' Sukie shouted. 'And above all else, that bloody woman needs to leave the castle. I can't stand the sight of her. Will's right, she's nothing but an imposter. Had your mother wrapped round her little finger all right, didn't she? Get her away from me, Eddie.'

I couldn't hear what Edward said in reply, but evidently Sukie's drunken tantrum was lessening, as her voice wasn't so shrill. In fact, both their voices were less clear now – presumably they were walking back to the house, having abandoned the car and its defunct battery.

'What the hell was all that about?' Jesse whispered after a while.

'Clearly me and the money,' I muttered back. 'Or maybe killing me to protect the money...'

'Shit,' Jesse said. 'This is really serious stuff, Grace.'

We waited a little longer, and then Jesse deemed it safe enough to turn his light back on. He took my hand. We walked off again, our mood sombre.

We went on and on, for what seemed like ages; Jesse shining the light in front of us, and us navigating roots, fallen branches and many tree trunks. Even with the beam of light it was tricky to keep going; it's one thing to walk through a wood in daylight, and quite another to do it in the black of night. So many twigs, bushes, brambles and branches impeded us, that I could feel my skin getting scratched even through my clothes. But we had to keep heading on; stopping and going back was absolutely out of the question. After a while, Jesse came to a halt.

'I think we're nearly at the lake,' he said, taking his hand away from mine. He walked off. 'Yes we are, we're nearly there, Grace. Come over here and I'll show you.'

I stumbled off in the direction of the light. But I could barely see around me now. More damn twigs scratched at my arms and face, and I had my hands up, trying to push them out of the way. God, this place was overgrown.

'That's it,' Jesse said. 'You're nearly here, Grace. I'm holding my hand out towards you, can you see it?'

I ran towards him, suddenly desperate to get out of the eerie dark trees. To be in a more open space again. That's when I tripped over something hard and roundish protruding up from the ground, completely losing my footing. I felt my ankle twist as I crashed down in the blackness. Pain shot through me.

'What the fuck was that?' I shouted.

Chapter Thirty-Nine

In seconds, Jesse was at my side, shining his torch around.

'I think you tripped over the entrance to the old icehouse,' he said.

'The what?' I said, rubbing my ankle, and swivelling it slowly about. My descent to the ground had worsened the ache in my head, and for a minute all I wanted to do was get back to some sort of – safe – dwelling and look at my injuries in the light. To find some strong painkillers and to rest my aching body. Just for a split second, my resolve wavered. I thought about giving up, and just taking the easy route and returning to London without pushing through and trying to get to the bottom of the weird mystery I was so unwittingly involved in. I'd never been a tough outdoor type, always preferred sitting at a desk with a book, or in the last few years, with a laptop. My time at the castle, and all the events that had unfolded, had pushed me so far beyond my comfort limit that for a second I struggled with how I was going to carry on. *No, Grace,* I thought. *Stop thinking like this. You're so close now. You'll have a lot of time for making things better later. Right now you need to put all the pain out of your mind, stay the course, and focus on finding where*

Archie's key fits. That's the only thing you can do right now to resolve all of this...

'They were popular before fridges were invented,' Jesse said, bending down and shining the light on my ankle. 'Loads of country estates had them built in the grounds, and I think the former gardener here said this one dates from around 1775. They were packed with ice and snow in winter months, which then kept perishable food cold for ages. Quite clever really.'

The pain in my ankle now subsiding, I looked around.

'Oh yes, I remember seeing it labelled on the maps in the castle,' I said. 'Can you shine the light on it? I've never seen one before.'

Jesse did. I could see the small brick bump that I'd fallen over. It was joined – by a tunnel-like structure – to a much larger mound that was several metres round and looked like a big brick igloo. The whole thing looked like it had sunk into the earth – it was covered in moss, lichen and weeds – and I couldn't see an entrance to it anywhere.

'How did they get into it?' I said.

'If you look at the bit that you just tripped over,' Jesse said, pointing to the smaller mound. 'You can see that the top of the door is still just about visible. Over the years, the earth has grown up around the icehouse, kind of consuming it. That's why it looks like it's being eaten by the ground. It hasn't been used for over a century. People didn't have any use for it after fridges were invented, because who wants to go traipsing all over the grounds to get meat when they can just open a door in the kitchen?'

'But would it have been used when Archie was alive?' I said, staring at the top of the old door. I bent down, and started scraping away the earth around it, feeling clumps of it get stuck under my fingernails. It was well and truly barricaded by years of soil growth.

'Possibly,' Jesse said, his tone doubtful. 'I mean, I know they had outdoor rooms for cheese and meat here back then. They're still there, although we use them for storage now. Howard and his friend once excavated around here, looking for Archie's treasure. Look, you can still see the big dents where the soil was filled in.' He shone the torch around, and I could see patches of earth that looked different to the rest. 'Even after they'd scraped a lot of the soil away they couldn't get the door open, it's made from strong wood and they couldn't find a key for it. So they decided to dig down next to the icehouse, and then upwards, hoping to get into it that way. From what Howard said, they didn't find anything in there. Another wasted search.'

'Hmm,' I said, still scraping away at the dirt with my hands. It was coming away in bits but it didn't seem that I was getting anywhere. The door was still half buried. Then one of my nails caught on something rough. 'What's that?' I scraped away a bit more. 'Jesse, look. It's a keyhole in the door. Where's the key that I gave you earlier? Let's try it.'

Jesse retrieved the key from his pocket, and handed it to me. I inserted it into the lock, and turned. There was resistance, and it was hard to move it, but eventually the key turned in the icehouse door.

Chapter Forty

'We've done it,' I said, excited. 'We've found the right door for the key. Wow.'

'Well done, Sherlock,' Jesse said with a grin, putting his torch down next to me so that the light shone upwards. Then he got on his hands and knees and began digging away at the dirt too. He seemed excited now. Then he stopped and turned to me. 'There's no way that we're going to be able to clear the earth away, it will take days if we try to do it by hand. We need to go back to my cottage and collect a shovel.'

But I carried on digging for a few more moments, not wanting to give up so easily, and then in desperation gave the top of the door a shove. It moved slightly.

'Woah,' Jesse said. 'Maybe there's no handle on it, just a lock. Do that again.'

So I did. The door moved inward a little more. Jesse got down on his stomach, and gave the door the biggest push that he could, using all his strength. Bit by bit, it opened inwards, revealing a dark open space at the top of the mound.

'Shine the torch in,' I said. As Jesse did this, we both leaned forwards, and saw what looked like a small tunnel, with a wide open space at the end of it. 'Do you think we can fit through the gap? Maybe go in and take a look round?'

'It will be tight,' Jesse said. 'But we might manage it. We'll have to make sure we can get out again though. We definitely don't want to get trapped in there – no one would know where we were to come and look for us.'

He stood up, and found a large branch that was lying somewhere on the ground. Using it as a kind of shovel, he swept away several more layers of earth from the icehouse door, until the hole looked like it was just about big enough for us to jam ourselves through.

'I'll go first,' he said. 'Then I can help you in. You've had a few knocks today, Grace, and you don't need any more.'

I held the light for him, appreciating his concern, as he squeezed himself through the hole, feet first. When he was through, he had to duck a bit, as the ceiling and door height was so low.

'Your turn now,' Jesse said, holding up his hands. In seconds, I was through, Jesse's phone clenched tightly in my teeth.

I passed it to him, and he shone the light around. I could see that we were inside some kind of smallish chamber. It was fairly narrow – we could just about stand two abreast – and the brick walls arched up into a low dome above us. At the end of the passage was a much larger space that plumbed down several metres. Parts of the wall had been knocked through, and lots of broken bricks, earth and rubble lay at the bottom of it. Weeds and moss covered most of them. It was clear from the state of the icehouse's insides that no one – other than us – had been inside it for years.

'That's where they must have kept the ice in the old days,' Jesse said, pointing down. 'I've seen pictures of other icehouses, they always had a big chamber for storage. And by the looks of it, that's also where Howard tunnelled into when he was looking for Archie's stash. No wonder he didn't find anything, he just burrowed into a large empty space and must have thought that there was nothing else there.'

'Jesse, look at this,' I said. I'd noticed that there was a door next to me, on the right side of the passage. 'What do you think this is?'

'No idea,' Jesse said. 'Is it locked?'

I grabbed the handle and turned it. The door started to open, but got stuck. Jesse stepped forwards and gave it a shove. As it opened fully, hinges creaking, we saw another dark space in front of us. Jesse shone the light into it.

'Looks like another small tunnel,' he said. 'That's odd. As far as I know, icehouses were just built with this large room here – so that food could be piled in and kept fresh. Maybe there's another space for storage down there...' Our eyes met, and I guessed that he was thinking the same thing as me.

'Let's go and have a look,' I said, stepping forward.

With Jesse shining the light over my head, I made my way along the tunnel, and reached some steps that had been carved into the earth and packed tightly. Going down them, Jesse close behind, I stepped out into a large space. It wasn't like the ice storage area, that had been like a big bubble carved down into the earth. This one was level, like a kind of earth cave. With the help of the phone's light, I could see an armchair, a rug, and a small wooden bookcase that was packed with boxes. A pile of papers sat on the top of it, with a mug on top of them.

I realised that I was holding my breath as I looked around.

'I don't think this was dug out by whoever built the icehouse,' I said, turning to Jesse. 'I think Archie excavated this room for himself. Probably as a kind of private area so that he could escape from his family and have some peace and quiet whenever he felt like it. They probably had no idea where he was, when he was down here. I already know – from reading his journals – that Cordelia often complained that he was spending too much time 'excavating old rubbish', as she put it. She didn't seem to have any understanding or interest in his archaeology hobby – in fact it just seemed to annoy her. He was probably often down here, getting away from her and her constant demands, and obsessive socialising. And in a letter to his friend Charles, he said he was storing the valuables in 'the dug-out one'. He must have meant this place. And Charles must have been a loyal enough friend to take the secret to his grave.'

'Yes, you might be right.' Jesse put his hand up to feel the packed earth on the roof of the cave. 'Wow, Grace. This really is an amazing find.'

'Let's have a look in these boxes,' I said, walking to the bookcase, feeling my hands tremble as my excitement levels sky-rocketed. 'If I'm correct, I think we might have just found something even more special in here. Not just Archie's cave, but some things that are altogether more valuable and that people have been searching for for decades...'

I took a box off a shelf, and opened the lid. Jesse shone the torch down. A pile of glittering jewels lay at the bottom of it, snaking together in a dazzling heap.

Chapter Forty-One

Diamonds sparkled from earrings, necklaces, bracelets and a tiara. A sapphire ring shone a deep blue, giant gold coins lay in a pile and what looked like a pearl and emerald ring sat on top of them. Pieces that I didn't recognise lined the box, some looked medieval, some even older. My thoughts spun as I gazed down at them. Could this really be happening?

'Shit,' Jesse said, exhaling. 'We've bloody found it. This must be Archie's hoard.'

Carefully placing the box to one side, I took another from the shelf and lifted off the lid. An ornate, gilded clock was inside, as well as a very old, grand-looking watch, a wooden globe, and several small figures that looked like they were made from bronze. Putting that box aside we looked through the others, finding such a wealth of priceless treasures that for a while we were both speechless. More jewellery, all of it dripping with diamonds, sapphires, emeralds, rubies and pearls. Brooches, ornaments, statues, ancient figurines, and many jewel-encrusted crosses. One box held a collection of swords and daggers, their hilts covered in tiny glittering diamonds.

'Jesus Christ,' Jesse whispered, reaching out but then hardly daring to touch the priceless artefacts in front of him. 'This whole collection must be worth millions. Billions, maybe. Must have been amassed by the Trengrouses over hundreds of years. It's unbelievable. I've never seen anything like it. Not even in a museum.'

'I know,' I said, feeling light-headed, my heart hammering in my chest. 'I can't believe we've found it. The family have been looking for all this for over a hundred years. And here it is, right in front of us. Archie left it stashed in his icehouse hideaway the whole time. And he did leave clues in his papers. Although they were quite obscure, and he'd hidden the important letters in the skull. He obviously wanted to make discovering these items as difficult as possible for everyone.'

'What do we do now?' Jesse said. 'There's no way we can take all this anywhere in the middle of the night by ourselves. There's too much of it, and if we started carrying these boxes out and back to my cottage one by one it would take hours.'

'No we can't do that,' I said, trying to think fast. 'We can't risk losing any of it. It's so dark outside now. And you're right, doing it by hand would just take us too long.'

'And on top of that it would be too dangerous,' Jesse said. 'Most of the family already seem furious that you're here, Grace, and there's a killer on the loose. If whoever is behind all this finds out that you're the one who found Archie's hidden treasures they will probably be out of control with rage. God only knows what they would do then. I can't even think about it. We can't let anyone know that they're here, and that we found them. If we're going to take all of this out of the icehouse to keep it safe then we need to do it quietly, and all in one go.'

I knelt there quietly for a minute, staring at the glittering stash in front of us, hardly able to believe my eyes. Everything that Jesse said was true. It would be like throwing a grenade at the killer, to publicly come out as the person who found the buried hoard. They were already incandescent with fury, and prepared to kill to protect the Trengrouse money and whatever else it was that was motivating them. If they realised that we'd found it then no doubt they would explode, and their subsequent actions would be unimaginable. There was no way that I could tell anyone what was down here. Even going to the police about it wouldn't be a good idea. They'd no doubt tell the Trengrouses straight away – after all – it was all on Godwyne's estate, and therefore legitimately theirs. And the killer might find out, come and take the hoard, and that would be the end of that.

My connection to Archie was complicated, and I didn't have absolute proof of it. Yet. But proving that I was directly related to him would be easy once I had access to online geological sites and any records my sister had kept. With my laptop and phone now stolen by whoever had attacked me, this wasn't something I was going to be able to do all that soon. Then a realisation hit me. A thunderbolt. The bloody thief had taken the bag with Beatrice's wedding certificate and Jacob's birth one in it. Fuck. Without them, it was going to be a whole lot more difficult to prove my birthright, even with all the knowledge that I now had. They'd been *my* key to everything. I needed them to prove that Beatrice was a Trengrouse, that Jacob had been legitimate, and they were solid pieces of evidence that I could track my own bloodline back to. Without this proof, the treasure would simply be handed straight to the Trengrouse family, and no doubt the killer would make off with it before it could be secured and dealt with in the right way. We'd done all of this for nothing.

'Shit,' I said, exhaling, a heaviness clouding my head. I explained what I'd just realised to Jesse.

'Oh God,' he said with a groan. 'I'm so sorry, Grace. You don't deserve any of this. And you were so close to being able to prove the truth. There must be something we can do? Some way of keeping all of this safe until Lady Alexandra's murderer is caught?'

'Yeah, I know,' I said, as a fog of depression pervaded my thoughts. 'But I have no idea what that is.' The pain at the back of my head, where the attacker had hit me, was throbbing. My ankle still hurt. And now everything I'd worked so hard to find was gone. An exhaustion overtook me, and I felt like lying down on the rug on the floor. What good was it to find Archie's hoard if I couldn't prove my connection to the family? Alexandra would have died in vain, murdered in cold blood by a ruthless killer who was prepared to go to any length to stop me from proving that I was a Trengrouse. Poor Mrs Taylor had been attacked, no doubt to stop her from telling me what she knew. I wouldn't be able to raise any money for Gabby and Penny, I wouldn't be able to help my niece get over to America for the treatment that she so badly needed to keep her alive. Without those certificates, everything was ruined. The murderer had won. I sagged as the last bit of my energy and resolve left me. I'd failed. Not just myself, but Alexandra and Mrs Taylor, Penny and Gabby.

I felt Jesse gently place a hand on my back.

'I'm so sorry, Grace,' he said softly.

I stayed bent over, cradling my knees, unable to move or speak. Everything we'd done to find the hoard that evening now seemed pointless. The key, the letters, trying to honour Alexandra's wishes – all futile. There was nothing I could do to make things right without proving that I was so closely related to Archie. All the research I'd done since hearing what Alexandra had to say on my first night at the castle, all the unnecessary violence, all the secrets, mysteries, lies and bad feeling amongst the staff and family. If we told anyone about finding Archie's hoard, then the whole lot would naturally go straight to the seven Trengrouses who currently lived at Godwyne. They would be so pleased, and would be able to carry on with their gambling, drinking, affairs and whatever else they did in secret. I was out of ideas. I was even too shocked by the realisation that everything had been ruined by the murderous attacker to cry. I exhaled, feeling the last bit of energy leave my body.

'Wait,' Jesse said, a few moments later. 'Grace, listen. I've had an idea.'

Chapter Forty-Two

I couldn't move or speak. Couldn't even acknowledge his words.

'Okay,' Jesse went on. 'This is a long shot, but it might just work. Like I told you, Derek Brentwood has always been on damage limitation duty for as long as I've worked at Godwyne. Whenever there's a hint of a scandal, he makes it go away quickly, so no one in the outside world knows what the Trengrouses are really like. Everyone just thinks that they are this fine upstanding family. But they're not, they are as messed up as can be, as you now know. You told me about your journalist friend, didn't you? Well, why not do the opposite of what Derek does. Instead of hiding and being a secret, why don't you go public with absolutely everything that's happened. Tell the world. Get it all out there.

'Get your journalist friend to write a story about how you came to Godwyne and got told by Lady Trengrouse that you're a direct descendant to Archie. How she then mysteriously "fell" out of a window. How you found the certificates, how a statue nearly fell on top of you, how Lady Trengrouse left you notes and a massive inheritance. How she thought it was terrible that

Beatrice and Jacob were disinherited, and wanted to right the wrongs done by Cordelia all those years ago.

'Your friend can tell everyone about the horrible letters you got, how someone went through your room, how you think someone's watching you on the CCTV, how the memory stick that recorded what went on on the night of Lady Trengrouse's death has conveniently gone missing. You can tell them about the attack on Margaret, just after she'd said she needed to talk to you urgently. If you're brave enough, you can say how revolting Will has been to you, and how the Trengrouses aren't the picture-perfect family they seem from the outside. You can talk about the attack on you, and how someone stole your bags and now they have the important birth and wedding certificates. You can tell everyone about your niece, Gabby, and how you and your sister desperately need to raise the funds to take Gabby for the treatment, and how that's largely been your motivation for trying to get to the bottom of this mystery. Then you can tell them about the legend of Archie's buried treasure, how Lady Trengrouse wanted you to find it, and how we actually did come across it in the icehouse's secret room. We can take loads of photos of it with my phone and send them to the journalist. Go public, Grace. Break through the family's wall of silence and tell your truth loudly to everyone.'

By now, I was sitting upright, Jesse's crazy words having ignited a tiny bit of energy in me.

'You're insane,' I said, looking at him in the torch light. 'Do you know that? If I can't prove what I'm saying, then the family can sue me for libel. Slander. They can say that I'm mad and made the whole thing up. I could even be arrested.'

'It's risky, I'll admit,' Jesse said, 'but I don't think you would get into trouble, Grace. Because once word about you is out, there will be many other ways to trace your inheritance. Everyone's doing it these days, with DNA tests and stuff. And I can be a witness, say I've seen the certificates. Once you've proved that you are who you say you are, no one can argue with the fact that you're a Trengrouse. And everyone will know your side of the story, even if the family contest it. They'll hate their business being so widely known about, but that's their problem. They won't be able to hide and scheme in secret behind the castle walls anymore. And once everyone knows what's going on, there will probably be a much more thorough investigation. The killer may well be caught. Who knows, the certificates might even be found.'

'But you might lose your job, Jesse, if they find out that you've been helping me,' I said, feeling more drive flood back through my bones. 'Are you really willing to risk that?'

Jesse paused for a minute, and then looked at me.

'Yes,' he said. 'I am. I really like you, Grace. I mean, *really* like you. And having seen you go through so much here at Godwyne, I want to help you get the truth out there. If you'll let me.'

I thought for a moment, and then nodded.

'If you're willing to sacrifice your livelihood then I guess I am too,' I said with a grin. 'I think your plan is ridiculous, far-fetched, precarious, and probably won't work. But it's also pretty amazing, and it's the best option I've got. And I have to say that I do like the idea of getting everything out in the open. There's too much subterfuge, too many lies here at Godwyne. And if it means I can finally somehow raise the funds for Gabby, then I'm willing to give it a shot. But I know the family may well try to stop me ever being given the inheritance that Alexandra left me. I can't rely on that. And anyway, even if I do get it – which would be totally amazing – it might take a year to come through, and I'm not sure my niece can wait that long...'

'I know,' Jesse said, rubbing his hands together. 'Now all you have to do is phone your journalist friend and convince her to write this bloody amazing story about you.'

'Yes, although Kim might say no,' I said.

'Well you won't know until you ask her,' Jesse said, holding his phone towards me. 'Here, use this. I have a couple of bars of signal down here, which should be enough.'

'Oh shit,' I said, taking the device. 'Kim's number's on my phone, which the person who hit me has got. Hang on, I might be able to find it another way.' I went on to Google and put in the words *'Kimberly Ulrich journalist'*. The internet was slow down in the cave, but eventually several articles that she'd written came up. And luckily her phone number was on the first one that I opened, under her name.

'Okay,' I said, exhaling. 'Here goes nothing.' I tapped on the number, and after a few seconds the ringing tone filled my ear...

Chapter Forty-Three

'Crikey,' Kim said, when I finally paused for breath. I'd filled her in on everything as much as I could, and was half expecting her to say that she didn't believe a word of it, because as I was explaining everything that had happened, it even sounded unbelievable to me. How could all of that have taken place in such a short space of time? I waited with bated breath to see what her reaction would be...

'And you can send me photos of the jewellery and treasures that you found tonight?' Kim went on. 'Christ, Grace. This is an amazing story. Horrific at times, but also mind blowing. It's front-page stuff, actually.'

'Really?' I said, feeling my excitement levels rise. 'Do you really think so, Kim? Would you be happy to write about it?'

'Yes,' Kim said. 'More than happy.'

'Oh, thank you so much,' I said, as excitement zipped through me. 'And of course I can send you photos of the hoard. We can send you one of the last awful note I received too, as Jesse still has that as we haven't had a chance to give it to the police yet.'

'Bloody hell,' Kim said. 'I don't think I've ever had a scoop this big. Great, I'll give you my email address, and if you can send all those photos through I'll contact my editor to let him know what's happening, then I'll start writing everything up. If you can email me a synopsis of everything you've just told me that would be helpful too, with as many names and dates as you can manage. And also links to the previous articles about Archie's buried hoard. The more evidence we can provide, the better.'

'Of course, I'll do that as soon as we've finished chatting,' I said. 'Thank you so much, Kim.'

She gave me her email address, and I typed it down on Jesse's phone in a blank message. Then we said our goodbyes, and rang off.

'Oh my God,' I said, looking at Jesse. 'I can't believe it. Good old Kim, she's actually going to help us get word out about this.'

'That's fantastic,' he said, grinning. 'Listen, I've been thinking. We can't stay down here indefinitely, apart from anything else we have no food or drink. Would you be okay staying here while I go and fetch my car? I'll drive it as close to the icehouse as possible, and we can load all the boxes into it, then go and stay somewhere safe until tomorrow. Not my cottage, that would be too risky. I'll drive us to a town somewhere and we can book into a hotel or B&B. That way, we'll be out of Godwyne when the story breaks. We can go to the police tomorrow, show them the letter, tell them about the attack on you, and show them this hoard. And also find a doctor to look at your head, just to be on the safe side. Although I must say, you're suddenly looking a lot brighter than you were about twenty minutes ago.'

'Yes, okay, I'll stay here,' I said, not liking the thought of being left on my own at all, but knowing that Jesse's plan was the most sensible option. My head and ankle were hurting a lot.

Plus, there was the issue of what to do with the treasure. 'Don't be too long though, will you?'

'I'll be as quick as I can,' Jesse said, reaching into his pocket and passing the horrible note that Zara had delivered to him earlier. He hesitated for a moment, then leaned forwards and gave me a kiss on the cheek. 'Don't worry, I won't let you down. I'll be back before you know it, and then we can head away from the estate, and find a nice safe place to stay for the night. You can keep my phone with you, and while I'm gone you can take photos of all this, and send Kim whatever she needs.'

'Sounds amazing,' I said, my cheek feeling rather tingly. I smiled up at him. 'Take care out there, won't you?'

'Oh don't you worry about me,' Jesse said, heading for the passage. 'I'm too big and tough to let anyone hurt me. Just let them try it, and they'll get more than they bargained for.'

I watched as he waved, then disappeared into the blackness of the small corridor. A wave of anxiety whooshed through me. *Right*, I thought. *It's just me, the phone, and Archie's hoard now. And I've got too much to do to hang around feeling nervous or scared. I need to get on with taking these photos. After all, Kim's got an important article to write...*

Chapter Forty-Four

After a few attempts, I worked out how to shine the light of the phone onto the piles of treasures, quickly taking a photo of them with the flash turned on afterwards. I'd arranged the goods along the floor of the earthen cave before I'd started, so that everything was shown off to the best possible vantage. As I snapped away, taking close-ups and also shots of the entire hoard together, I could hardly believe what I was doing. Like so much of what had happened since I'd arrived at Godwyne, this felt like a dream. I mean, could we really have just found Archie's buried hoard? Was I actually in a small dug-out room with it, taking photos to send to my friend Kim? It was all mind-blowing stuff. The constant pain in my head and the now lesser ache in my ankle were the only reminders that yes, this was a very real situation.

After I'd taken a good collection of photographs, I sat down on the floor again and set to work. First, I composed an email to Kim, detailing as many names, places and incidents that I could remember. I photographed the nasty note that Zara had delivered earlier, and attached that image to the email. Then I added a good selection of the photos of the hoard, and sent the whole lot to my wonderful journalist friend. I checked the sent folder, just to make sure it had all safely zoomed away to Kim in cyberspace, and sure enough the message was showing as having been successfully despatched.

Right, now I just had to be patient and wait for Jesse to come back. But as I sat there, shining the light of the torch in front of me – aware that I'd just seen that the battery on his phone was very low now – the icy fear returned, creeping through my veins incrementally. What if Jesse took ages, and the phone died? I didn't honestly think that I could cope with sitting there in the cave by myself in the pitch black with no light. I'd coped with everything that had happened at Godwyne in the best way that I could, made myself go on and keep forging ahead in order to find out as many truths as I could. But – although I hadn't told Jesse – that attack had really taken the energy out of me. Had exposed my vulnerability in a way that nothing ever had before. And if the phone battery died and I had to endure sitting with my thoughts in the darkness, well... I wasn't sure I'd be able to deal with that at all...

Get up and look around the cave, Grace, I told myself. *Focus on other things.* I'd always found that distraction was a wonderful tool when my thoughts were going into overdrive, and now was the ultimate time for testing that coping mechanism. I stood up, brushed myself down, and went over to Archie's old bookcase. If I could just immerse my interest in whatever was on there, then maybe the biting terror that was building in my mind – at being alone down here when there was a killer on the loose – might subside a bit...

Picking up the dusty old papers from the top shelf, I angled the torch light down so that I could take a look at them. The first was a hand-drawn family tree, and after my time spent in the library I recognised the handwriting immediately. It was Archie's. His and Cordelia's names were in the centre of the page, and above them were the titles and names of both their parents and grandparents. Below his and his wife's names, Archie had written; Beatrice, Ottilie, Lettie and Alice. John Stewart's name had been inserted next to Beatrice's, and Giles Fitz Duncan next to Ottilie's. Then below Beatrice and John's names, Archie had put Jacob James Stewart, and Emilia Zara Stewart.

Hmm, I thought, looking up for a second. *Zara is an unusual choice of name, I thought it was a more modern one. I didn't realise children were named that a hundred years ago. And what a coincidence, that there's a Zara working at Godwyne today. Unless...*

Big building blocks of understanding began plummeting into my brain.

'No, surely not,' I whispered. 'She can't be...'

A noise behind me made me jump and I nearly lost my hold on Jesse's phone. I turned quickly, flashing the light in front of me.

Zara was stepping down into the earthen room.

Chapter Forty-Five

'You?' I said, my voice still a whisper.

'Hello, long-lost cousin,' Zara said, the light making her eyes flash bright. 'So you found Archie's buried secrets, did you? Very clever. I've been looking for them myself for ages, but it looks like you've done me a favour by finding them first. I did hate getting my nails all dirty, so thank you for that. I won't have to do any more digging.'

'But...' I said, too shocked to think clearly. 'Why are you working here as an accountant if you're related to Archie? Surely you could have just told the Trengrouses?'

'Oh sure,' Zara said, sarcasm entering her voice. 'Just rock up to the castle one day and announce that I'm their long-lost relative, without a shred of written evidence to back up my claim. All I had was the knowledge that my dad told me, and a family heirloom that's been passed down since Emilia's time, an old Bible with her name at the front of it. I've searched the heritage sites – saw you on there actually, with your sweet little claim to being related to the family in some way. But I never put anything on myself, there was no point. Anyway, it doesn't look like the surprise announcement with the family has worked too well for you, Grace. Alexandra seemed to like you, but I can't say the same for the rest of them. You should have heard what Sukie was saying to Edward and Will the other day. You're definitely not her favourite person; in fact I would go as far as to say she can't stand the sight of you.'

'No,' I said. Oh God, surely this couldn't be happening, not when we'd got this far... 'I may have put in a vague connection to the Trengrouses on the ancestry sight, Zara, but it was more for fun than anything else. I didn't know I was directly descended from Archie and Beatrice until I arrived here, and Alexandra told me. I honestly had no idea before that. All I knew – from an old family legend – was that I was somehow related to the Trengrouses, probably ten times removed or something. I didn't come to Godwyne with any other agenda than to write a book.'

'Of course, whatever you say, Grace.' Zara's eyes narrowed. 'Play the dumb, innocent card if you want, but I reckon you just came here because you were after the money. Why else would you be walking around at night looking for this treasure?'

She stared at the glittering stash on the floor next to me, and a greedy look came over her face. There was no point in me trying to justify my arrival at the castle, I could see that Zara had no interest in understanding the truth. A shot of anger pulsated through me.

'So you were the one who listened to my conversation with Alexandra?' I said, my voice getting stronger. 'It was your footsteps that I heard hurrying away. And it was you who pushed her out of the window and killed her?'

'I'm afraid so,' Zara said, her gaze snapping back to mine. 'Couldn't have the old girl helping you out like that, could I? God knows why she took such a liking to you. But once I realised that she had, and that she was trying to help you understand your connection to the family, that was that. She had to go.'

'And then you took the USB stick that contained the CCTV recordings from that night,' I said, feeling disgust as I looked at her. 'To hide the evidence of what you'd done. You absolute coward.'

'Yes of course I did,' Zara said, sneering. 'I'm not exactly stupid, Grace. The police didn't pick up on anything when they watched the video, but a shadow of me was on there and I didn't want anyone else looking at it. I wasn't about to leave a trail of clues lying around that led back to me, was I? I've been watching you on the cameras in the office since you first arrived at Godwyne. Saw you poring over the documents, and scribbling your notes. It was me who wrote those letters to you, me who pushed the statue on you. It was meant to be a warning, a sign telling you to bugger off back to London, but if it had killed you I wouldn't have minded. It was me who ordered Alexandra's room to be cleaned so quickly, although I told everyone that the order had come from one of the Trengrouses.

'But you ignored all of my warnings, didn't you? If you'd been a bit smarter, you would have listened to them and saved your own skin by pissing off back home. Instead, you decided to stay here like some sort of heroine, and try to solve all the mysteries in Godwyne. I think writing books has gone to your head. You seem to believe in fairy-tale endings, when they're just a load of made-up shit. In fact, you've been nothing but a massive pain in my side since you arrived at the castle, Grace, if I'm honest. Always getting in the way, and being the interesting new arrival who messes everything up.'

'But why are you doing all of this?' I said, as Zara reached into her jacket pocket and pulled out something shiny and pointed. A large knife.

'Because I want to get back what is rightfully mine,' Zara

said. 'You don't need any money, Grace, no matter how much you play the victim card. You're a well-known writer. I mean, how hard up can you be? If you need some cash for your niece then take out a loan like a normal person. *I'm* the one who deserves the hidden wealth here. *I'm* the one who's really had to struggle, because of the big fuck-up that Cordelia made all those years ago. Not you. You've never had to fiddle the books in businesses you work for just to get by, have you? If Beatrice had been allowed to stay in the family, I'd never have gone through what I have. Never have lived in such poverty when I was a child, never seen my dad become an alcoholic, never have had to struggle to bring myself up like I did, without anyone else to rely on, or to look after me.'

'Listen, Zara,' I said. 'I'm so sorry to hear that you've had a hard time, I really am. But things have been tough for me too. Like you know, my niece Gabby...'

'Oh shut up, Grace,' Zara said, spitting out each word. 'I've had enough of listening to your self-pitying talks. You're the successful one. You'll find a way to make your life work out. I owe hundreds of thousands to a debt company. Hundreds. Of. Thousands. I've been charged with fraud. Can you get your head around that, Grace? I'm in serious trouble. I'm not like you, Miss Perfect.'

'But...' I said. 'How? Why?'

'Because I didn't come from a nice little loving family like you,' Zara said, her eyes venomous. 'I didn't have a sister, mum and dad who loved me. My parents were fuck-ups and they dragged me down into their world with them. It took me years to claw my way back out, and start trying to become a better person. I know I don't look like I come from that kind of background now, but do you know how many years it took me to separate myself from all of that? To reinvent myself as *successful Zara*? And if Beatrice had stayed a Trengrouse, none of that would have ever happened. I'd have been born into a much better world. I need this money so badly. I've got into trouble, and I've lost everything. I need to use these treasures to get back to where I belong in the world. To wipe out my past troubles, and to start again. I'm desperate, Grace. I even staged a break-in at the castle last year, trying to frighten the family into thinking that someone was after them, as much as I was trying to find out information in that bloody library about where the treasure was. But that was a bloody disaster when the security guard turned up and I had to make a run for it.'

'But look how you managed to overcome all the hardships in your life,' I said, staring at the knife she was holding. 'You're an accountant, Zara. A successful one, if you got a job here. You don't want to throw that all away and mess up your whole career just because of a fuss over a bit of money, do you?'

'I'm being sued, Grace, by my former employers,' Zara said. 'Not by just one company, but by two. Obviously the Trengrouses know nothing of that, as I used a different surname when I started working here – Moore. My real name is Zara Kelly. Got people I know to sort out the references. It wasn't that hard. I've got jobs in that way before.'

My mouth was hanging open. I couldn't believe what I was hearing. Could this really be happening? Zara, the nice accountant at Godwyne, was the murderer of Alexandra?

'And I suppose you attacked Mrs Taylor too?' I said. It was my turn to spit out the words. Knife or no knife, what this woman had done – the damage she had wreaked just for money – made me incensed. An image of Mrs Taylor lying there unconscious on the floor with blood oozing from her head flashed through my brain. My free hand curled into a fist.

'Yes, of course,' Zara said. 'I had to, obviously. Didn't I? If only Margaret had kept her nose out of everything she would still be okay today. Not lying in a coma in the hospital.'

'So she's not dead?' I couldn't help asking.

'No,' Zara said. 'Not yet, anyway.'

'You really are a vile piece of work,' I said, shaking my head, wondering when the best time to smack her would be. Maybe I could take her by surprise and pull the knife out of her hand? 'You wouldn't need this treasure so badly if you hadn't scammed so much money from those businesses. It was your choice to act like that, but you clearly can't handle the consequences. You've made other people suffer, trying to get what you want. Look at the mess you've made here at Godwyne. Stop blaming your childhood and Beatrice for everything and take some bloody responsibility.'

'Yeah,' Zara said, stepping forward. 'Easy for you to say, you're someone who's never had it hard, Grace. Listen, don't make this more difficult than it needs to be. I'm going to take everything here and leave Godwyne, I have my car parked nearby, so I'll just load up and get out of your hair. Stand aside, will you? There's a good girl.'

'How did you know where to find me?' I said, desperately playing for time, my eyes on the knife, my fist still curled. 'How did you know I was down here with this hoard right now? If you've been looking for it for ages, how did you suddenly know that I'd found it here tonight?'

'Ah.' I saw Zara sneer in the torch light. 'I've been watching both of you on CCTV. Keeping an eye on your movements. I knew you were up to something this evening, so I followed you. As a result, I saw Jesse when he came back outside. He didn't exactly tell me that you were down here with all this, but – as I've said – I'm not exactly stupid. There would be only one reason that you guys would be out at night...'

'And why were you wandering around in the middle of the night in the first place?' I said, as Zara got even nearer to me. 'Bit weird, isn't it?'

'Bit of a hypocritical question, isn't it?' Zara said with a laugh. 'I was actually driving out here because I needed to get rid of something.'

'What?' I said. Then realisation struck me. 'Whatever it was you used to hurt Mrs Taylor with?'

'Well done, Grace,' Zara said. 'Maybe you're not as stupid as you look after all. The statue that shattered when I pushed it on top of you became very useful. I took a large chunk of it in case it ever came in handy. And as it turned out, it did.' She was moving from one foot to another now, and I could see in her eyes how desperate she was for this wealth. How anxious she was that her plan worked out.

'I wouldn't do anything too hasty to me right now,' I said, watching her hand that was clutching the knife rise upwards. 'Jesse is going to be back here any minute...'

'Ah,' Zara said. 'Now that's where you're wrong, Grace. Jesse won't be coming back here. Sadly, he's rather incapacitated right now, what with one thing and another.'

'You bitch,' I said, stepping towards her and raising my arm. 'What the fuck did you do to him?'

Zara laughed. It was an ugly sound.

'Just made sure he wouldn't be able to come charging back here to save his little princess,' she said. 'That's all. Now come on, step aside, Grace.'

As I stared into her eyes, all of the emotions I'd felt when I'd seen Alexandra's body lying on the ground came welling back up in me. Anger, sadness, grief, frustration. I'd promised Alexandra that I would get to the bottom of things, and I'd done that. I'd found Archie's buried hoard. She hadn't died in vain. And this woman – some sort of cousin of mine – had the cheek to say that I didn't need the money as much as her? That because she'd scammed a business and got into trouble, she deserved it more than anyone else? My sister's voice – crying –

as she told me that Gabby was so ill that she'd gone back into hospital, began playing around in my head. It was Gabby and Penny who deserved to benefit from these treasures. Saving Gabby's life was more important than anything else. Than anyone else. And I was going to see to it that that's exactly what happened.

'No,' I said quietly. 'I'm not moving. You're a bad person, Zara. You don't deserve to benefit from any of this wealth.' I stepped forward, bringing my fist down towards the knife.

Zara's eyes lit up with fury. She lunged forward, knife held out in front of her.

'We'll see about that, you pathetic little cow,' she hissed.

She was too quick for me. I was already injured, and my reflexes weren't what they could have been. The last thing I remember was watching the blade of the knife sliding between my ribs, the blood immediately oozing out onto my shirt, the searing pain.

Then blackness...

Three days later...

Jesse's head appeared round my hospital cubicle curtain.

'Grace?' he said. The worry lines on his forehead seemed to have increased since I'd last seen him. Which wasn't surprising, all things considered. 'Can I come in?'

'Yes of course,' I said, smiling at the sight of him. Then I saw that he was moving slowly, as though he was in pain. My smile disappeared. 'Are you okay, Jesse? What did Zara do? When she came down into the icehouse cave she told me that she'd attacked you, as she didn't want you coming back to stop her taking Archie's hoard.'

'Yes, she gave me a nice big bump on the head just after I'd finished talking to her,' Jesse said with a grimace. 'I'd just started walking back towards my house – as I was going to pick up my car, wasn't I? – but then I saw a car stopping next to me, and Zara got out. We had a quick chat, said goodbye, and I continued walking. Then she must have attacked me, because I don't remember much after that. When I woke up, I had a face full of dirt. Must have crumpled right down where I was standing. As soon as I woke up, I crawled back to the icehouse to see if you were all right, but she'd stabbed you by then. She ran off when she saw me, so I grabbed my phone and called an ambulance. My head's okay now, I just have to move around slowly and then it doesn't hurt too much. Motion seems to make me feel a bit dizzy. But I'm all right. I got off lightly compared with you.'

'Mm,' I said, touching the spot where the bandage under my vest top wrapped round my ribs. 'Yes, she certainly did her best to harm me with that knife. But sadly – for her – she managed to miss all my organs. Just. I fainted in the cave because of blood loss and shock apparently. Although if you hadn't shown up when you did I think she would have finished me off completely. Zara's a nasty piece of work. She's evil. I feel ashamed to be related to her.'

'Have you heard what happened to her?' Jesse said, sitting down on the end of my bed.

'Yes, Detective Paynter came to see me yesterday,' I said, shifting a bit to get comfortable. 'He told me about what happened. Sounds completely crazy. He said that she ran to her car, after you'd disturbed her in the icehouse, and drove away. But the police immediately put out a nationwide BOLO to be on the lookout, and she was picked up trying to board a ferry in Portsmouth. She was taken back to Cornwall and the police fingerprinted her and realised that she was actually the con woman whose face has been splashed all over the papers.

'He said that they've found out that Zara has a criminal history, having previously been charged with defrauding two businesses. She was deeply in debt when she realised that she was a direct descendant of Archie. When she found that there was apparently buried treasure in Godwyne's grounds – probably from researching the family on the internet and finding old newspaper reports – she made an effort to move close to the family. She thought she couldn't use her real name, in case they looked her up and found out that she had a criminal past. So she made up a surname and somehow got the job of accountant. She had no proof of her connection to the Trengrouses, so didn't tell anyone about it. Her plan – apparently – was to find the buried hoard, and to sell it to raise funds. Seems she truly thought she was entitled to it. She'd been working on her plan for over a year, and had even staged a break-in to throw the family off her scent the year before, when she tried to get into the library to find documents that might lead to the whereabouts of the treasure. She was furious when I arrived, especially when Alexandra took a liking to me. She saw me as direct competition for the wealth she felt that she deserved and decided to eradicate the trail that connected me to any possible inheritance.'

Jesse shook his head.

'I just can't believe it,' he said. 'Zara always seemed so nice when she was working at Godwyne. So normal. Always stopped for a chat. Although now I look back on it, I did find her wandering around the grounds on her own quite a lot. I just presumed she liked being outside in nature. I just can't understand how someone who can act like that can also be a murdering criminal.'

I sighed.

'Yeah,' I said. 'I know what you mean. Detective Paynter told me that she's probably a psychopath, and can use charm when she feels like it. But then she can also be ruthless and violent when she wants, and feels no remorse about anything she does.'

My sister, Penny, had taken time away from Gabby to come up to the hospital and see me the day after I'd been taken in. I'd called her to explain what had happened, once I was safe and stable, and she'd screamed and said she was going to get on a train to Cornwall, that Gabby was doing okay, and that she'd explain to her that Auntie Grace was poorly and needed her to visit. I'd told her about everything that had been going on at Godwyne, and we'd laughed, cried and hugged. It was hard telling her about everything that Zara the psycho had done, but I knew I needed to be honest with her, and give her the whole story. My sister could hardly believe it when I told her about the inheritance that Alexandra had left us – obviously I planned to give as much of it to Penny as she needed. And she was even more incredulous when I got to the part about finding the hidden treasures.

I'd reassured her that all this new-found wealth meant that we would definitely be taking Gabby over to America for treatment very soon, at which point we'd both laughed and cried until we were exhausted. I'd been sobbing with relief, as well as because of the trauma of the previous few days. Relief at being able to reassure my sister that Gabby would get the treatment that she needed, and relief that I'd actually been able to honour Alexandra's last wishes, and bring some resolve to the wrongdoings at Godwyne. The old lady hadn't altogether lost her life in vain – Zara had been unveiled to be the awful human being behind all the destruction, Archie's hoard had been found, I'd been told about my connection to the family and was now a part of the Trengrouses – albeit in a new and strange way – and the family's secrets and lies would now be more difficult to hide away. Although none of this could ever bring her back, it made me feel better to know that I'd gone some way to meeting her wishes, and to bring the goings-on at Godwyne out into the open.

'The whole thing is insane,' Jesse said. 'But I'm just so glad that you're okay, Grace.'

I grinned.

'Thanks to you,' I said. 'You saved my life, Jesse. I don't know how to make it up to you.'

'Agree to come out for dinner with me when you get out of hospital,' Jesse said. 'That will be enough for me.'

I nodded.

'It's a deal,' I said. 'Oh, and I've had some really great news. After what you told the police and everyone about me being directly descended from Archie, you know – the night that I was stabbed – Kim ended up telling a solicitor she's friends with. They did some researching of their own. They found direct records that show my sister and I descend from Beatrice and Jacob, and they emailed them to the Trengrouses at Godwyne.'

A big smile spread across Jesse's face.

'And I bet they were absolutely delighted by that news,' he said with a chuckle.

'Well, I doubt Sukie was,' I said, grinning. 'But Howard popped over yesterday afternoon and said that arrangements must be made to include Penny and I in everything that goes on in Godwyne. And he also said that a share of Archie's treasure will go to me and my sister. Most of it is being given to a museum in Truro, which is absolutely the right thing to do with it. It seems that him and Mimi were quite pleased that I'm their close relative. So it looks like – if I can sell a couple of bits – I'll be able to send Gabby to America for treatment fairly soon. When she's well enough to travel.'

Jesse leaned forwards and enveloped me in a big hug.

'I'm so pleased, Grace,' he said, his words muffled by my hair. 'It looks like things are going to be okay for your niece after all.'

'Yes, I hope so,' I said, hugging him back.

'Have you heard about Margaret?' Jesse said, eventually leaning back a bit.

'Mrs Taylor?' I said. 'No, what's happened?'

'She woke up yesterday,' Jesse said. 'And guess what the first thing she said was?'

'What?' I said.

'She said: "Zara did it". She must have seen the woman coming for her before she was knocked unconscious.'

'Oh thank God she's going to be okay,' I said, feeling tears sting my eyes. 'I've been feeling so guilty about not going to talk to her straight away when I had the chance. I should never have gone to your cottage to dump my bags, I should have gone with her to see what she was so bothered about.'

'Hey,' Jesse said. 'It wasn't your fault that Zara's a psycho, Grace. So don't start blaming yourself. None of us could have known what she was up to, could we? And anyway, Margaret is apparently sitting up in bed now and talking, and has even eaten a small meal. So she'll be fine. I'm going to pop in and see her later.'

'You're a good man,' I said.

'I do my best,' Jesse said, with a wry smile. 'You'll never guess who I ended up having a drink with last night?'

'Who?' I said.

'Only Howard.' Jesse shook his head as though in disbelief. 'I think we both needed one, after everything that's happened. He came over to talk to me when I was sitting on the mower, unable to do much work as my head was aching. Suggested I go back to his rooms for a pint, which turned into several. He's a nice chap actually. And I couldn't believe what he told me, once he had a couple of beers in him.'

'What?' I said, sitting up a little straighter.

'Only that his mother and Will have both finally agreed to get help for their alcohol addiction,' Jesse said with a smile. 'Apparently their alcoholism has been like an elephant in the room for the family for years. Always there but never spoken about. Well, with all that's happened and come out in the open, Howard took the opportunity to address the issue with both of them. Said he'd had enough of it and that if they wanted to stay at Godwyne they would need to agree to get help. Which they did, eventually. He's been put in charge of the Godwyne estate for now. It seems as though the family's natural instinct to hide all their vices is now going to be cleaned up. He said it was Sukie and Edward that Margaret overheard talking, and that they weren't on about killing anyone, they were discussing getting you away from the castle. So that clears that little mystery up. No doubt Mr Brentwood will still be on guard – trying to minimise any hint of scandal – but at least, in private, their problems are being acknowledged and dealt with.'

'Wow,' I said. 'Good for Howard.'

'Yep,' Jesse said. 'He also said that the family suspected that Lady Alexandra's death wasn't an accident, but that Mr Brentwood had strongly advised them to say that she'd just wandered off and fallen out of a window by herself, in order to keep the whiff of scandal away from Godwyne. Howard said that he wasn't happy about this, and even wondered if Mr Brentwood was behind the murder and the attack on old Margaret. Said that Derek *does* get paid more than all the other members of staff and didn't want the castle or the family to come to ruin – probably protecting his job and his hefty wages.'

I shook my head.

'I thought it was Mr Brentwood behind everything too,' I said. 'The way that he looked at me sometimes, and the fact that he had the CCTV in his office, and because that memory stick went missing, and the way we overheard him talking to poor Mrs Taylor, telling her not to go to the police with what she knew. But it never crossed my mind that Zara had access to the memory stick and CCTV too. She always just seemed so harmless and nice. It's scary to think how deceived we can be by appearances.'

'Yep,' Jesse said. 'I know what you mean about Zara. And I was wondering about old Derek in the end too. In fact I was pretty sure he had something to do with it. But his weird behaviour must just have been because he was worried about how to minimise the growing scandal at the castle. Oh, and Howard told me a bit about the affair that he had a while ago.'

'Blimey,' I said. 'Sounds like you had a right old chinwag.'

'Yes, we got on really well actually,' Jesse said. 'And the beer helped. He's a good chap, the best of the lot of them. Seems that several years ago him and Mimi were going through a rough patch, and he had a one-night stand with an old girlfriend. But that was it, he wasn't a serial womaniser or anything. Him and Mimi managed to get themselves back on track and sort their marriage out. Seems that village gossip didn't get it right about Howard, he's a decent bloke.'

I nodded.

'Good,' I said. 'I instinctively liked and trusted him the most. I'm glad he's a good egg, and it's great that he'll be in charge of the estate from now on.'

'What are you going to do about your book?' Jesse said. 'You know, the one you've been researching ever since you arrived at the castle?'

'Ah,' I said, feeling a smile creep across my mouth. 'I've actually had an idea about that. Given the press interest in the crazy story, I thought I might pen my own account of everything that's happened. Turn it all into an autobiographical account. You'll be given a star part too, especially as you found the hoard as much as I did.'

'That's such a good idea,' Jesse said. 'And obviously I'm up for having a starring role in the whole thing.'

I laughed.

'Old Mary's pleased,' Jesse said. 'Because Hobnob finally turned up after going missing for two days. Mary thinks she must have seen Zara attacking Margaret in the castle hall, and have been so upset by it that she scarpered away across the fields. She's been out round the grounds shaking Hobnob's favourite treats and calling her name for ages. But then apparently, she woke up yesterday morning to find the cat sitting on her doorstep like nothing had happened.'

'I'm so pleased she's come home,' I said. 'I did see her running away from the castle just before I found Mrs Taylor lying there on the floor, but with everything that's been going on, I forgot all about her. She is a lovely cat.'

Jesse nodded.

'Oh,' he said, reaching for his bag. 'I almost forgot. I brought these to show you, Grace.' He pulled out a couple of newspapers and placed them in front of me.

Long Lost Heiress Finds Lord Trengrouse's Buried Treasure, the headline of the top one said. *Must have been written by Kim,* I thought. *I owe her big time for this, bless her.* I read on, and found that what followed was a rich account of how Jesse and I had stumbled upon Archie's hoard in the icehouse, complete with photos. I had to admit it was a great article, Kim had really pushed the boat out with this one. When I'd finished reading, I had a big smile on my face. I was out in the open as a Trengrouse now, there was no turning back. The whole country – or readers of this paper anyway – would know my connection to the family. And although it was a bit scary, it felt brilliant that I wasn't just a secret to be hidden anymore, I was 'out' as Archie's descendant.

I pulled out the other newspaper from underneath. Heir to Fortune Turns Killer, was the headline. 'Zara Kelly – otherwise known as Zara Moore – duped the Trengrouse family from Godwyne Castle,' I read out loud. 'Kelly had previously found out that she was a descendant of Archie Trengrouse, but after she was arrested for defrauding a company she was working for three years ago, she decided to masquerade as an accountant to gain employment at the Godwyne estate. This was allegedly because she didn't think they would accept her if she gave them her real name, given the criminal charges already against her. Kelly had become aware of an old family legend; that Lord Archie Trengrouse had buried treasure worth millions somewhere in the grounds of Godwyne Castle. Believing herself to be entitled to this hoard, but feeling unable to be honest about her connection to the family, Kelly managed to gain employment as the Trengrouses' accountant, and spent many nights digging for the treasure. But when another long-lost family member showed up – Grace Haythorpe – Kelly felt threatened.

'Despite her best efforts, she had been unable to find the secret stash. And she was horrified when Grace was quickly accepted into the family by the now deceased Lady Alexandra Trengrouse. We have learned that after eavesdropping on a private conversation between Grace and Lady Trengrouse, Kelly felt compelled to take action. Lady Trengrouse was found deceased outside the castle shortly after Kelly overheard her and Miss Haythorpe's conversation, apparently having fallen from a window. A day later, the housekeeper – Margaret Taylor – was brutally attacked and left for dead. Kelly has now admitted to being responsible for both the murder and the attack on Mrs Taylor, and faces charges of murder and attempted murder.

'In a twist to the story, it was Grace Haythorpe who eventually found Archie's buried treasure in an old icehouse in the grounds of Godwyne Castle. Shortly after her discovery, she was attacked by Kelly – who wanted to take the riches for herself – receiving a stab wound to the stomach. We understand that Miss Haythorpe is currently in a stable condition in hospital.

'The Trengrouse family have released the following statement: "We are shocked and saddened to hear about the actions of Zara Kelly. We would have welcomed her into the family with open arms, had she come to us and relayed the nature of her connection to the family. But instead she chose a wicked route as she attempted to gain the family's fortune. Grace Haythorpe is the heroine of the story, and we are delighted that she discovered Archie's buried hoard, and that she is such a close – albeit long-lost – relative of ours. We wish her a speedy recovery and look forward to seeing her at Godwyne again once she is better".'

'Wow,' I said, looking up at Jesse. 'The Trengrouses have formally recognised me as a close member of their family.'

'Yep,' Jesse said with a grin. 'Miracles do happen.'

Then his expression changed, and he looked a little sad.

'I suppose you'll be going back to live in London after this,' he said. 'When you're out of hospital?'

I couldn't help grinning.

'Oh, I don't know,' I said. 'I'm starting to like it in Cornwall. And there's still that meal you've promised to take me for... so... I might stick around for a while and see how things go.'

'I think that's the best idea you've ever had, Grace Haythorpe,' Jesse said, as his face brightened again. 'Tell me, will it hurt your stitches if I lean forward and give you a kiss?'

I laughed.

'Well there's only one way to find out...' I said.

THE END

Also by Sarah Sheridan

THE SISTER VERONICA MYSTERIES:

The Convent (book one)

The Disciple (book two)

The Tormented (book three)

Devil's Play

Girl in Bed Three

A Perfect Family

The Temptress (novella)

The Ghostwriter

A note from the publisher

Thank you for reading this book. If you enjoyed it please do consider leaving a review on Amazon to help others find it too.

We hate typos. All of our books have been rigorously edited and proofread, but sometimes mistakes do slip through. If you have spotted a typo, please do let us know and we can get it amended within hours.

info@bloodhoundbooks.com

Printed in Great Britain
by Amazon

24059563R00128